What Reviewers Say About Bold Strokes Authors

KIM BALDWIN

"'A riveting novel of suspense' seems to be a very overworked phrase. However, it is extremely apt when discussing Kim Baldwin's [*Hunter's Pursuit*]. An exciting page turner [features] Katarzyna Demetrious, a bounty hunter...with a million dollar price on her head. Look for this excellent novel of suspense..." – **R. Lynne Watson**, *MegaScene*

"*Force of Nature* is an exciting and substantial reading experience which will long remain with the reader. Likeable characters with plausible problems and concerns, imaginative settings, engrossing events, and a well-tailored writing style all contribute to an exceptional novel. Baldwin's characterization is acutely and meticulously circumscribed and expansive." – **Arlene Germain**, reviewer for the *Lambda Book Report* and the *Midwest Book Review*

RONICA BLACK

"Black juggles the assorted elements of her first book, [*In Too Deep*], with assured pacing and estimable panache...[including]...the relative depth—for genre fiction—of the central characters: Erin, the married-but-separated detective who comes to her lesbian senses; loner Patricia, the policewoman-mentor who finds herself falling for Erin; and sultry club owner Elizabeth, the sexually predatory suspect who discards women like Kleenex...until she meets Erin." – **Richard Labonte**, *Book Marks, Q Syndicate, 2005*

"Black's characterization is skillful, and the sexual chemistry surrounding the three major characters is palpable and definitely hot-hot-hot.. If you're looking for a more traditional murder mystery, *In Too Deep* might not be entirely your cup of Earl. On the other hand, if you're looking for a solid read with ample amounts of eroticism and a red herring or two, you're sure to find *In Too Deep* a satisfying read." – **Lynne Jamneck**, *L-Word.com Literature*

ROSE BEECHAM

"...her characters seem fully capable of walking away from the particulars of whodunit and engaging the reader in other aspects of their lives." – *Lambda Book Report*

ROSE BEECHAM (CONT)

"When Jennifer Fulton writes mysteries, she writes them as Rose Beecham. And since Jennifer Fulton is a very fine writer, you might expect that Rose Beecham is a fine writer too. You're right… On the way to a remarkable, and thoroughly convincing climax, Beecham creates believable characters in compelling situations, with enough humor to provide effective counterpoint to the work of detecting."
– *Bay Area Reporter*

GUN BROOKE

"*Course of Action* is a romance…populated with a host of captivating and amiable characters. The glimpses into the lifestyles of the rich and beautiful people are rather like guilty pleasures… a most satisfying and entertaining reading experience." – **Arlene Germain**, reviewer for the *Lambda Book Report* and the *Midwest Book Review*

"*Protector of the Realm* has it all; sabotage, corruption, erotic love and exhilarating space fights. Gun Brooke's second novel is forceful with a winning combination of solid characters and a brilliant plot."
– **Kathi Isserman**, *JustAboutWrite*

JANE FLETCHER

"*The Walls of Westernfort* is not only a highly engaging and fast-paced adventure novel, it provides the reader with an interesting framework for examining the same questions of loyalty, faith, family and love that [the characters] must face." – **M. J. Lowe**, *Midwest Book Review*

LEE LYNCH

"There's a heady sense of '60s back-to-the-land communal idealism and '70s woman-power feminism (with hints of lesbian separatism) to this spirited novel—even though it's set in contemporary rural Oregon. Partners Donny (she's black and blue-collar) and Chick (she's plus-sized and motherly) are both in their 50s, owners of the dyke-centric Natural Woman Foods store, a homey nexus for *Sweet Creek*'s expansive cast of characters.…Lynch, with a dozen novels to her credit dating back to the early days of Naiad Press, has earned her stripes as a writerly elder. She was contributing stories to the lesbian magazine *The Ladder* four decades ago. But this latest is sublimely in tune with the times. " – **Richard Labonte**, *Book Marks, Q Syndicate, 2005*

Visit us at www.boldstrokesbooks.com

TRISTAINE RISES

TRISTAINE BOOK THREE

by

Cate Culpepper

2006

TRISTAINE RISES

ISBN 1-933110-50-3
THIS TRADE PAPERBACK IS PUBLISHED BY
BOLD STROKES BOOKS, INC.,
NEW YORK, USA

FIRST EDITION: BOLD STROKES BOOKS, INC., AUGUST 2006

CREDITS

EDITORS: CINDY CRESAP AND SHELLEY THRASHER
PRODUCTION DESIGN: J. BARRE GREYSTONE
COVER ART: TOBIAS BRENNER (http://www.tobiasbrenner.de/)
COVER GRAPHIC: SHERI (graphicartist2020@hotmail.com)

By the Author

The Clinic: Tristaine Book One
Battle For Tristaine: Tristaine Book Two

Acknowledgments

Warm thanks to my editors, Cindy Cresap and Shelley Thrasher. I also appreciate the inspiration and advice of my friends Jay Csokmay and Dana L'Wood. Radclyffe has assembled an immensely talented stable of writers and creative staff at Bold Strokes Books. I'm grateful for all the support they've given the Tristaine series, especially Lori Anderson and Connie Ward in promotion, and Tobias Brenner and Sheri for their great cover work. As always, thanks to my adanin on the Tristaine mailing list, for all their patience and support.

DEDICATION

In memory of my friend Elaine K. Allen

*Beyond our ideas of right-doing and wrong-doing,
there is a field. I will meet you there.*

— Jelaluddin Rumi

CHAPTER ONE

Motionless, it watched the two Amazons. Bitter drool overflowed its withered lips and dripped to the stone floor. Acidic steam rose where spittle hit rock. It hadn't fed in generations.

❖

Jess's scruffy mustang shifted beneath her, one hoof clocking against the stony ground. She soothed the horse and scanned the deserted village. Her fingers drifted to the hollow of her throat and the light, welcome weight of the turquoise pendant resting there. Brenna's gift. A beautiful, rough stone the color of cold seawater, secured by delicate copper wire to the thong about her neck. Touching it eased the tightness in Jess's shoulders.

Bracken pawed the rocky earth again, grumpy in the twilight stillness.

"Shut up, ye crab. We're about done." Jess tousled her mount's thick mane. She released a low whistle and a moment later heard the distant trill of Vicar's response. She nudged Bracken into a canter toward the center of the village to meet her cousin.

"Nothing." As fair as Jess was dark, Vicar sat her tall roan with a lazy ease that bespoke years astride Tristaine's mountain herds. "This camp is deserted, Jesstin. Nothing on two feet has tracked over this ground in our lifetime."

"Get patrols to search every cabin." Jess eyed the stone altar that seemed to mark the mesa's geographic center. "And Shann and the others come no closer until we check the woods on all sides."

"Aye, easily done." Vicar grinned and crooked a blond eyebrow. "You think madlady Artemis has forgiven her tiff with Tristaine at last, Jesstin? Amazon luck is changing. Call the odds of finding this village. Even made by our own kin, by the look."

"But what clan?" Jess narrowed her eyes in thought. "Amazon archives don't mention any of our sisters settling so high in these mountains."

"Jess, our glyphs are everywhere."

That much was true. The village square was surrounded by rough log cabins of various sizes, in mixed states of repair. Crude Amazon glyphs were carved above the threshold of each.

Jess felt her gaze drawn again to the small stone altar. Carved deep on its craggy surface were the same timeless symbols of war, hunting, mothering, creation, and worship common to all clans claiming Amazon blood.

"I count enough lodges for most of us." Vicar uncorked her canteen and took a generous swig. "And enough timber on these hills to build more, once the snows lift. Plus a strong stable. It'll be hard labor, but we'll need that by spring thaw. We'll be restless."

"I'll be content to get us through the winter alive, Vic." Jess shook her head to decline the canteen.

"We're not likely to find better shelter." Vicar leaned over and spat delicately. "And none too soon. We'll be up to our silky butts in snow by next moon. Amazon luck, Jesstin. Changing at last. Our Brenna deserves the credit. She finally charmed Tristaine's spirit guides into sending the dream that led us here."

"Ah. She's *our* Brenna now, when she finds us an abandoned village. She's only *my* Brenna when she dumps a haunch of venison in the cooking fire."

"Aye, then she's yours."

"You've warmed to her, then." As always in their private conversations, Jess heard her own brogue deepen to match Vicar's more pronounced burr. "I wasn't sure you would, adanin. You're stubborn about City girls. Among all other things beneath Gaia's moon."

Vicar shrugged. "By my lights, your lady's earned her lodge with us, City-born or not. Brenna saved your neck in our last battle, Jesstin. She's a good healer, a decent seer. Horrific taste in lovers, but a strong heart."

"That she has." Jess shivered and pulled the high collar of her sheepskin jacket against the back of her neck. The sensation of being watched was as palpable as cold fingers drifting up her spine.

"What?"

"I still feel eyes." Jess shook her hair off her forehead. "I know we've covered the mesa twice and found nothing."

"Then what's the...?" Vicar sighed. "No. Go on, Jesstin. Dyan swore by your instincts, and you've proved her trust. I want to mind your gut."

Jess nodded toward the circle of small cabins ringing the square. "What happened to the Amazons who built this village? Why did they leave the mesa?"

"Plague?" Vicar scratched her scalp and shrugged. "One harsh winter too many? We'll never know, Jess. But it's perfect for Tristaine." She swept her arm in a slow arc. "These forests are flooded with game, and a mesa's easy to defend. Care was put into its design, and it was forested well." She pointed toward the expanding circles of poplar, aspen, maple, and oak that surrounded the village. "It's a natural fortress."

"Aye." Jess sat still for a long moment. "We've seen

enough for now. Let's find an easier trail up that rise. Something wide enough for the wagons."

❖

It watched the light woman canter after the dark one, the hooves of their horses kicking up the sparse dust of the square. Its dripping eyes followed its prey until it was out of sight, and the hunger in its blood surged.

The love between these two mortal Amazons ran deep, but it was more than equal to the challenge. The stronger the bond, the more devastating the betrayal. It gathered its sleep-logged energies and reached out.

❖

The mesa looks like the top layer of a round cake, with trees for candles, plopped down in the middle of a valley, Brenna wrote. She sat cross-legged on a small hill overlooking the pasture, her journal balanced in her lap.

We've laid camp in the field I dreamed about, surrounded by thick forest. The mesa looks out of place here, in the midst of all this open land. It seems pathogenic, like a raised birthmark that might prove malignant. The Amazons find it strange too, and I trust their instinct over mine. But they think this odd landmark might be some kind of blessing from their goddesses, a gift to our weary clan. I'll have to take their word on that. I never left the City limits before I met Jess, so my knowledge of divine intervention and mountain terrain is pretty nil.

As I remind Shann every time she insists on relying on my bizarre dreams to guide us through these stupid mountains.

The Amazon word for mountain is "hill." Much like Jess calling that canyon we leaped over to escape the flood a "ditch." When Shann said we'd have to go deep into the hills to find a new site for Tristaine, she meant hauling six hundred women, kids, and assorted livestock over a bloody range of sheer cliffs.

Brenna had already filled half of her notebook with the chronicle of that journey, which had taken all summer. The clan had endured long weeks of pure, grueling effort climbing a harrowing series of mountain passes. Moving always higher, farther from the City and the watery grave that drowned their last village.

Her journal described Shann's calm leadership throughout their migration. Even when a fast, cruel fever swept through their tribe in high summer, taking some of Tristaine's youngest children and vulnerable elders, Shann's courage kept her women's spirits kindled with hope.

Shann's authority was tempered by her humanity. Brenna remembered watching tears pour soundlessly down Shann's face as she cradled a dying child, her refined features fixed in an eloquent expression of grief. The image had stayed with Brenna, and she'd sketched the two figures at the bottom of one page in her journal.

She focused again on her entry.

It'll be dark soon. We've finished laying camp, so I can sit here for a few more minutes, imagining disasters. Bracken threw Jess and she fractured her skull. She and Vicar have been jumped by grizzlies. They've been ambushed by a City patrol. Unlikely, I know, but they should have been back hours ago.

What other horrific fates can befall two Amazon warriors on an uncharted malignant birthmark? Caster came back from the dead and turned them to stone. Homicidal bandits captured them, or a swarm of rabid bats chased them off a cliff.

I used to panic when my little sister was ten minutes

late from school. I'm not sure my nerves can stand a lifetime married to an Amazon warrior.

Brenna scanned the pasture below her, a waving blanket of silver in the twilight. She willed two small moving dots to appear at the base of the shadowed mesa, but the vista remained stubbornly empty. Blowing her bangs off her forehead, she bent over the lined notebook again.

I last saw my sister just days before I helped Jess escape from the Clinic—sweet Gaia, over a year ago. I wish I remembered the last thing I said to her. I do remember the last thing she said to me—that sisters shouldn't treat each other the way I was treating her. Sammy was four months pregnant. If she's alive, I'm an aunt by now. But if Caster was telling the truth, Sammy is dead.

Brenna rested the pen gently on the notebook. Her hands ached to cup Jess's shoulders, their broad strength always a source of comfort. The atonal humming of crickets rose around her, and she shivered in the cool evening air. As if on signal, a warm cloak plopped over her head like a tent. She smiled in the sudden green darkness. "Gee. Thanks, Shann."

"Don't mention it. I'm used to chasing foolish children who sit out in cold open fields, wearing no cloak to speak of, with night coming on." The queen of Tristaine was well into her fifth decade, but she curled onto the ground next to Brenna with the grace of a girl. "Stop worrying, Blades. A thorough scouting takes time. They'll be back soon."

"You're right." Brenna pulled the cloak off her head, static electricity crackling through her hair. "Did you have a chance to talk to Kyla, lady?"

"She helped me serve the stew." Shann leaned back on her hands, her gray eyes thoughtful. "There wasn't much talking.

She's still not able to speak of Camryn without tears."

Brenna nodded. Images of Cam's death still tightened her own throat without warning.

"But it seems Kyla's grief is taking a normal course, Bren. She's young and resilient. Her stillness doesn't worry me. She'll have time to heal, be it weeks or decades."

"You've been there, lady." Brenna watched the other woman's face.

"Oh, lass, I was a royal mess." Shann's smile held a note of resonant sadness. "I walked around like a zombie after Dyan was killed. I was all but unable to function, and the clan knew it."

"I don't think I could rule a tribe of wild women after a loss like that." Brenna pulled the cloak around her shoulders, trying not to imagine grizzlies or compound fractures. "Much less think clearly enough to get them through a crisis."

"An Amazon queen rules when she must, adanin." Shann's fingers brushed through Brenna's hair. "Whether or not she feels she's capable of it isn't usually a consideration, I promise you."

Let's not go there tonight, Brenna thought, her eyes closing at the gentleness of Shann's touch. Then a quiver of relief ran through her, and she sat up.

"Finally!"

"What? Ah." Shann smiled and stood. "Yes, here they come! And look, Brenna, both of them are dressed warmly. Fancy that."

Vicar and Jess loped through the high grass, riding shoulder to shoulder across the open field. Brenna stood next to Shann, brushing pine needles from her journal. She could feel Jess's exhilaration, even at this distance, in the rhythm of Bracken's swift rocking beneath her and the expanse of sky overhead. She wondered, not for the first time, how her lifemate had survived months of imprisonment in the City.

The Amazon cousins were incapable of riding side by side without racing, so they indulged in that pleasure for the last quarter league. Vicar's roan, Talos, edged out Bracken with a small but undeniable lead, and held it long enough to claim victory.

The horses were still nearly at top speed when Vicar reined sharply, then threw herself off her mount. She crashed bodily into Jess with enough force to knock her off her horse and hurl them both into the high grass.

Brenna felt the impact in her teeth, and for a moment she was immobile with shock. Then she jumped to her feet and raced down the gentle slope of the hill, reaching automatically for the stethoscope that hadn't draped her neck since she left the City Clinic. She heard Shann bark out an order behind her toward the camp.

To her immense relief, she saw Jess rise unsteadily from the waving grass, her hand clasped to the back of her head. She took a staggering step and dropped to her knees, and Brenna's heart jagged painfully in her chest. But then she was close enough to see she was kneeling by Vicar's still form.

"Hey." Panting, Brenna came to a sliding halt beside Jess and clenched her arms tightly. "You all right?"

Jess nodded vaguely, her eyes on Vic. "What the bloody hell happened to her, Bren?" Jess was breathless and a little pale, but seemed basically intact.

"Let me see." Brenna nudged Jess gently aside and laid her hands on Vicar's sides. Her breasts rose with shallow but steady breaths, and her pulse beneath Brenna's measuring fingers beat a rapid cadence.

"There's no blood." Jess scanned the field for any threat and clenched her cousin's collar with unconscious force.

Brenna was relieved to see she was right. There was no bleeding or other obvious signs of trauma. She felt the back of Vicar's head carefully, then bent closer. "Vic, can you hear me?"

"Vicar!" As usual, Jess opted for a more assertive approach. "You open your eyes. *Now!*"

Vic stirred beneath Brenna's hands, and her eyes opened. She blinked up at Jess's pale features.

"I'm in hell," Vicar croaked.

Jess blew out a breath. "Perverse wit intact. She'll be fine, Bren."

Shann reached them just as Vicar was lifting herself on her elbows.

"Blades? Are they—?" Shann stopped short, relief in her eyes. "Well, it seems they're still among the living. I expected to find one of you poleaxed, at the very least!"

"I'm all right, lady." Jess got to her feet, and Brenna watched her with a hawk's sharpness. Her own heart was only now calming from tympani speed to a more bearable rhythm.

"Aye, me too." Vicar winced and accepted Jess's hand up. "Beat you by more than a head, Stumpy."

"Move slowly, please." Brenna steadied her. "We want to make sure everything's still attached, so hold on to me until your head clears."

"Did Talos misstep?" Shann looked past them at Vicar's trembling roan, who stood only yards away.

"Is he hurt?" Vicar craned to see past Jess. "Why's he shaking like that? No, lady. Talos didn't throw me. Something knocked me flat."

"Aye, me too." Jess scrubbed the back of her neck. "You."

"Come again?" Vic frowned.

"You smacked me butt over beanie, mate. You sure Talos didn't find a gopher ho—"

"I don't fall off horses, Jesstin." Vic shivered hard and shrugged her leathers around her shoulders as she looked around the darkening pasture. "I told you, something hit me. Felt like a bloody elephant."

Brenna met Jess's troubled gaze.

"Whatever this force was, it's disappeared as suddenly as it arrived." The calm assurance in Shann's tone soothed Brenna. "We'll scout the field thoroughly at first light. For now, Blades, let's get these bruised wanderers to a warm fire."

"I'm for that, lady," Vicar grumbled. "It's colder than Caster's tit out here."

"Shann!"

They turned to see two Amazons on the low hill at the edge of the camp carrying a pallet between them. One held a smoking torch over her head, and Brenna realized it was fully dark.

"Stand down, sisters. We're all right." Shann's clear voice carried well in the pure mountain air. She slid her arm through Vicar's. "Come on. We'll want a closer look at you both before we ply you with Aria's excellent stew. Your report can wait until after you've eaten."

Brenna waited, shivering a little while Jess retrieved the reins of the two horses. She put her arm around Brenna's shoulders as they followed Shann and Vicar up the grassy rise to the camp.

"You're sure nothing's bent?"

Jess grinned down at her. Given her penchant for risking life and limb, the greeting had become a joke between them.

"I'm fine, querida."

"Kind of odd about Vicar."

"Well, Vic's odd."

"Jesstin." Brenna squeezed her waist. "Seriously. She hit you with a full body tackle. I saw it happen."

"Aye, I felt it happen." Jess turned to look back toward the mesa gleaming in the moonlight across the field.

Brenna nodded toward the mesa. "Did you find anything bizarre up there?"

"No." Jess frowned and brushed Brenna's upper arm

with her rough palm. "But it's a damn eerie village, Bren."

"Really?"

"Deserted, as far as we could tell. Very old. And... strange. That's the best I can do."

"Lovely. A haunted village. We've had so little excitement." Brenna rested her head on Jess's shoulder as they entered the camp, craving the bonfire Shann had mentioned. It wasn't really cold enough to justify her shivering, but she couldn't seem to stop.

❖

It had a terrible patience, born of silent decades craving Amazon blood to slake its thirst. It sensed that the generations of waiting were drawing to an end at last.

The passion uniting these mortals would be rendered poison. That's how it would conquer them, how it had defeated two other clans, long before these women were born. It would make them spiritual cannibals, preying on their own kind, as their sisters did.

It had turned the light one against the dark one effortlessly, even at this distance. That was its particular genius, corrupting the love between women into a toxic weapon. These Amazons were ripe for it. Its time was coming again.

It settled into its coffin and slept.

❖

"I can't restrain myself, lass. It's yer cute poutin' lips—"

"Jesstin." Brenna blew her bangs out of her eyes and glared into Jess's blue ones, inches above her. "These tents are made of paper!"

"Grrraded canvas." Jess's brogue twirled the words. "And it's a *prrrivate* tent." She bent her head again to kiss her.

"Squished up against fifty others." Brenna put a finger on Jess's nose to stop her. "And sound carries."

The journey into the hills had been difficult in more ways than one. Whenever Tristaine settled in one place for more than a few days, they laid camp to provide reasonable privacy. While traveling, however, safety took precedence over comfort, and the entire clan was assembled in one half of the large meadow. Brenna had yet to adjust to anything extremely personal in close quarters.

"Just who do you fear might be listening, lass?"

"Everybody."

"Who do you think would possibly object? Half the tents in the camp are rocking on their pegs, any given night."

"I *know*," Brenna muttered. "That's how I know sound carries."

"Welp, we'll get drowned out in the roar of the orgy, then."

Jess timed it well, her lips meeting Brenna's before she could respond, and after a moment, she began to relax beneath her. Her shoulders eased back against the blankets as Jess tasted her, a soft, sweet exploration of lips and tongue.

Then Brenna let her head fall back, and the kiss ended with an audible, wet pop.

"Look, remember, I lived alone in a single unit for five years, okay?" She tapped Jess's chin sternly. "I'm still not convinced that civilized people engage in wanton carnality in communal settings."

"Ach, City girls." Jess groaned and toppled sideways, sprawling on her back. "May Gaia grant the deprived wenches more carnality, please."

Brenna rolled on top of her long, lean form, and Jess

whoofed in protest. "Maybe we should keep looking, Jess."

"You're still fretting over this mesa, Bren? I doubt we can justify that, not with snows coming." Jess blinked at her. "Are you picking up anything clear about the village?"

"You make me sound like a metal detector." Brenna sighed. "No, nothing clear. Just a vague uneasiness. Like I've tried to tell Shann, I'm not sure when I'm sensing something or just having a fit of the creeps."

"It was your senses that helped us escape the valley with our lives, adanin." Jess's long fingers brushed through Brenna's hair. "You saw the flood before it wiped out our village. You saw Caster's attack before her soldiers found us. You saw a crossbow bolt headed for my chest and saved my life before it struck."

"I didn't see it in time to save Camryn," Brenna murmured. She laid her fingertip on Jess's lips. "I know. I just get nervous with Shann basing all her plans for Tristaine on what I *think* I see. I dreamed about this mesa, and we found it right where I thought it would be, but…what if it turns out to be a dormant volcano that goes undormant or something?"

"We'll pitch Vic in. A sacrifice to appease the gods." Jess's hands coasted over the planes of Brenna's back, then moved beneath the thick quilt to cup the swells of her hips.

"It would just be nice if Tristaine could stay put for awhile." Brenna rested her chin on Jess's sternum, shifting slightly as strong fingers began to knead her shoulders. "We don't want to go through all this again next winter."

"Tristaine has always been a wandering tribe, Bren." Jess tickled the backs of her thighs, and she tittered. "Amazons have always moved deeper into the wilderness as the Cities spread and grew. On this continent and others."

"You know, almost everyone in the City still believes Amazons are a myth." Brenna smiled, and Jess lowered her head to nuzzle her throat. "Lord knows I didn't believe in you guys until a certain criminally insane Amazon warrior was assigned to my ward."

"Better watch out for us psycho-butch Amazons." Jess lipped the smooth skin between Brenna's neck and shoulder, warming it with her breath. "We can be bloody irresistible."

"Jesssssss…" Brenna felt her nipples rise, two volcanoes nowhere near dormant. She listened to the quiet night around them, biting her lip. Maybe the women and children in the surrounding tents really were asleep, but they might just be eavesdropping in courteous silence. "You know how… enthusiastic we get. And loud."

Jess rolled again, carrying Brenna with her, and resumed her neck nuzzling from above. "I promise, lass, I'll restrain meself."

"It's not—*hoo*—it's not you I'm worried about…"

"I'll restrain you too." Jess laid a wet line of kisses along the taut skin of Brenna's throat, then moved lower.

"Jesstin. Jesstin. Honey? You know I'll…oh…*Hoo!* You know I'll do *that*. Jess, come on, everyone will hear."

"Brenna." Jess lifted her head and peered down at her. "You're really telling me I can't make love to you because you're afraid you'll make too much noise?"

"Will you lower your voice, please? I have been *trying* to tell you that for—"

"*Ah, sweet goddess, yes!*" Jess yelled. "Brenna, *yes, more*, you wild *banshee*."

"*Jesstin!*" Mortified, Brenna struggled beneath her, trying to clamp a hand over her mouth.

"Yes, there, *again!*" Jess pinned Brenna's flailing arms and bayed, "*Yes, again*, there. Ah, Brenna, you hot-blooded *demoness o' loove*…"

"*Mmrf onna ill oo!*" Brenna bucked like an outraged dowager, then heard a swift footstep outside their tent. She froze in horror.

"Everything all right in there?" Hakan's deep voice projected clearly as she rapped one knuckle on the tent's support pole. "Jesstin, you need help?"

Brenna could picture the master of Tristaine's stables waiting outside—grinning, her white teeth flashing against the beautiful ebony of her skin—then ducking neatly when Jess's boot flew out through the opening in the canvas and sailed over her head.

They heard Hakan snort laughter as she strolled on through the sleeping camp, continuing night watch. There were some faint claps and one sleepy whistle from the adjoining tents. Jess was chuckling, too, until Brenna clamped her fingers around her throat.

"I am so close to widowhood," Brenna snarled, her heart pounding hard between her still actively volcanic nipples.

"I'll comfort you, ye bereaved bairn." Jess kissed her again, smothering her squealing protests.

Brenna thrashed for a while, almost sincerely. No was no, after all, and Jesstin had just subjected her to public mortification, but, oh sweet lord, now she drew her tongue into her mouth and possessed it, sucking gently.

The strong length of Jess's body eased down onto Brenna, pinning her to the thick quilt. The hands that gripped her wrists slid them to either side of her head and held them there. Her thrashing slowed and became a sensual twisting so subtle Brenna was barely aware she was doing it.

Jess obviously felt the change, however. She could be a tender lover, and often was. She could also be aggressive and was then, blending power with gentleness, her hands moving thoroughly over Brenna's languid body. Winter clothing impeded her progress somewhat, but mountain Amazons were accustomed to undoing laces with cold fingers.

And after all that fuss, Brenna uttered hardly a sound beneath her lover's practiced touch. She crested in near silence, so robbed of breath that crying out was never an option. Her sighs merged with the natural rustlings of the sleeping camp, and Brenna fell asleep with Jess's breath warming her hair.

By the time Brenna watched Selene coast in full glory across the skies three nights later, the women of Tristaine were settled for the winter on the forested mesa.

CHAPTER TWO

Hakan, *get* your broad black butt out of my face!"
Similar cheerful taunts rang through the closely
packed forest as two hundred Amazons ran the perimeter of
the mesa. Vicar and Jesstin were hardly alone in their penchant
for competition. The daily training of Tristaine's warriors often
ended in a mad two-mile race around the boundaries of their
new home.

Small round leaves nicked at Brenna's face as she darted
through a copse of aspen. She raced up to another dense shrub,
lengthened her stride, and cleared it easily.

"*Karaki*, stepped right in *pendeja* moose shit again,"
someone yelled off to her left, and Brenna heard raucous
laughter. She mentally added attack by moose to her list of
certain calamities.

The pace was brutal and she was tiring, but it was one
of those glorious late-fall mountain days that still dazzled her
after twenty-odd years of breathing City smog. She wouldn't
have thought it possible to sip pure oxygen like wine, but on
days like this Brenna felt drunk on it. Now her lungs pulled in
great cold gusts of air, and vapor plumed between her lips.

The first time Brenna saw leaves turn with such startling beauty was last fall when she had entered the village of
Tristaine with Jesstin for the first time. That lush valley now
lay at the bottom of a vast mountain lake, and its Amazon
daughters were exiled to the high hills. But even if the Amazons

of Tristaine were as cursed as legends claimed, they seemed an inordinately fortunate clan now.

Brenna's foreboding about their new home still lingered, but she seemed to be alone in her misgivings. Even Jess shared the clan's general sense of relief and weary celebration now. Tristaine was starting to claim this land as her own. Forests were sacred to Amazons, and the rings of trees encircling their village were seen as a protective blessing.

The greenery Brenna ran through was thick with fragrant conifers and held a diverse and flourishing population of small game. She heard the rustle of escaping vermin all around her. Chipmunks and rabbits, she hoped, rather than some species of rabid mountain rat.

She slapped through the last few hanging willow branches and emerged, gasping for breath, into the village square.

"You bested half the guild, Bren!" Jesstin slapped her on the back, nearly toppling her to the thick grass. Brenna knew Jess kept her pride in her growing physical prowess low-key most of the time. As Shann's second and leader of the guild of warriors, Jess had to appear impartial.

Brenna perched her hands on her knees and panted like a spent hound as the rest of the field came jogging in from the forest behind her.

"Do you need to throw up?" Jess asked politely.

"Stay c-close. I might." Brenna hooked a finger in Jess's belt so she'd be sure to hit her boots if she did. All of this escaping from the oppressive City to live among free Amazons was nice, but it seemed to involve nausea-inducing adventures on a regular basis: getting gassed by City soldiers, dangling from a torn sash over a gaping chasm. Stuff like that.

Still bending, she saw two beaded doeskin slippers step into her field of vision. "Hello, Hakan."

"Young Brenna." A large hand patted the back of her head. "Drop something?"

"Ha and ha," Brenna gasped. "I like your slippers."

"A birthday gift from Kas," Hakan said. "I came to tell you the storyfire's lit, adanin, and Kyla's calling the tale tonight."

"Aye, sister, thanks." Jess smiled. "We've missed Ky's voice."

"That we have."

They moved toward the throng of Amazons gathering in the center of the square. The sun was just touching the timbered horizon to the west, throwing warm, golden light over the village.

Shann had said they were taking root again, drawing sustenance from the beauty and peace of the mountains. Brenna tried to share that optimism. For the life of her, she couldn't put a finger on her own nebulous worry about their new home. She kept sifting through her journal each evening, returning to the sketch she'd made of Shann cradling a dying girl in her arms. But sad memories aside, Brenna could find no new cause for alarm.

Vicar seemed none the worse for wear. She still maintained some phantom power had pitched her off her horse, and Brenna had no problem believing that. Vic had no earthly reason to attack Jess. Their bond was rock solid. And lord knows Brenna had learned to be a little more receptive to the whole arena of phantom powers. But perhaps now she could stop chasing demons that weren't there and relax a little.

"...and next time I will, you City sewage."

The venom in the voice made them turn. Brenna recognized Sirius, one of Jess's best archers, surrounded by a circle of warriors. An immensely powerful Amazon the color of burnished mahogany, Sirius looked rigid with anger.

Jess walked toward them, her step unhurried, and the warriors parted at once to let her in. Brenna followed, noting the palpable and growing tension in the group.

"Sirius, I ran nowhere near you."

Brenna lifted herself on her toes to see over Jess's shoulder, and her heart sank. Dana, the City mercenary new to their clan, faced down Sirius's angry glare with a look of sullen weariness. Both women still panted from the training run, and their breath shot bursts of steam in the chill air. There was a sudden flurry of motion, and Brenna saw Dana stagger, propelled by an abrupt shove.

"Kimba's bile," Jess grumbled, and moved so quickly Brenna almost fell. Jess darted between her two warriors and strong-armed them apart.

"Cool off, Amazon!" Hakan shouldered her way into the circle and swept one long arm across Sirius's chest, keeping her clear of the silent City soldier.

"Keep Caster's lapdog out of my path when we train, Jesstin!" Sirius shook Hakan off and spat into the dirt between Dana's booted feet. "Or I'll kick her into a ditch myself."

"You'll stand down, Sirius." Jess jutted her chin toward Dana. "What's this about?"

Dana returned Jess's appraising gaze without comment.

"This little girl almost kicked Sirius's legs out from under her, Jesstin," a warrior called from the back of the group.

"Oh, demon's bile, Lucia. She did not," another voice called. "Jess, if anything, Sirius lunged into Dana. I was right behind—"

"I've no interest in hearing children take sides in a playground spat." Jess's tone was calm but withering, and the circle quieted again at once. She turned to Sirius and regarded her silently for a moment.

"This is unlike you, sister." Jess rested her hand on the back of her powerful neck. "Dyan was always able to look to you for a cool head. I count on that now. We all do."

Sirius dropped her eyes, and the rigid lines of her body relaxed. "I hear you, Jesstin."

Brenna sighed softly, but kept her gaze on Dana. She had been a soldier under Caster's command when Tristaine's mountain village was taken. Her last-minute defense of the Amazons had earned her a home among them.

But just as Brenna herself had not, at first, been welcomed by every Amazon in the clan, there were warriors who couldn't forget Dana's past. The part of Brenna that still felt like a newcomer ached at the lonely pride in the young City woman's features.

"Tristaine lost nearly twenty daughters in the flood, adanin." Jess lowered her voice, which had the effect of drawing the ring of Amazons closer to her.

"We saw sister turn against sister. The bond between kin severed. Amazons shedding Amazon blood." Jess shook her head. "The waters cover that sad history now, and we'll not relive it here. Understood?"

"I hear." Sirius raised her eyes again, her dignity restored. "I do. It won't happen again, Jess."

Jess nodded and swept her gaze over the watching women. "Go on, you gawking horde. Join the storyfire before your butts freeze."

The small group dispersed as quickly as it formed, talk and laughter rising among them again. Brenna wrapped an arm around Jess's waist as she joined her.

Women and children, dressed warmly in soft skins and robes, were gathering in the center of the village square. The music of a dozen accents calling greetings to each other filled the night with a friendly warmth.

Brenna had learned to relish Tristaine's diversity of race and language, a blending of ancestries unheard of in the sterile homogeneity of the City. The clan's medley of ethnicities was matched by the complexity of the Amazons' faith. They worshipped an array of deities, all unique manifestations of the Feminine. Tristaine's culture blended the histories and folklore of a dozen nations, and her lifeblood was richer for it.

Women were spreading furs and thick rugs on the sparse grass around the storyfire, which crackled brightly in an open space near the ancient ebony altar. Kyla stood alone next to the shooting flames, and Brenna felt her throat tighten.

The Kyla she had met after escaping from the Clinic had still been very much a girl in her endless optimism and the buoyancy of her spirit. Kyla's delicate features still carried an almost fey beauty that belied the new stiffness in her slender frame.

The first night Brenna entered Tristaine, Kyla had sung an Amazon dirge of such beauty, she still effortlessly recalled every note. The woman who waited for her sisters to gather tonight had aged far beyond her years.

Her voice hadn't lifted in song since her wife Camryn died, and she wouldn't sing tonight. She was a spinner of tales now, and apparently the crisp fall air called for something ghostly.

"Her ravenous spirit rose again from the dank and sour mists of the underworld," Kyla began, her melodic tone quieting the square. "Called to profane life, the eater of Amazon souls…the Banshee's dark and more sinister sister…the queen Botesh."

Eager murmurs rose around the storyfire's circle. This was one of the clan's favorite ghostly legends.

Brenna settled against Jess with a sigh, her warmth welcome against her back. Like many of the Amazons around them, they sat on thick blankets that shielded them from the prickly grass of the square.

She turned her head on Jess's breast and saw a toddler nestled in her mother's arms a few blankets over. The little girl's eyes widened as Kyla continued her recounting of the increasingly gruesome tale.

"Before her pitted soul joined the leagues of demons,"

Kyla chanted, "Botesh walked the earth as ruler of an Amazon tribe. Queen of betrayals untold, she sucked the spirits of her own clan dry and left her sisters' lives in ashes. She shed the blood of her warriors in torrents, all in service of her depthless craving for dark power."

Brenna felt a chill trickle down her spine. Dyan's blood sister was a natural storyteller, and the fanciful spell she wove scratched at the comforting shields of logic. Even Brenna's City science-trained logic, which was formidable. Something in Kyla's dreamlike expression disturbed her, and she glanced over at the toddler hiding her face against her mother's arm.

"Hey, this is child abuse." Brenna nudged Jess. "That poor kid's gonna have nightmares for weeks."

"Probably." Jess nuzzled Brenna's hair with her nose.

"Really, Jesstin, it's not cool to scare little kids." Brenna had firm opinions on this subject, sculpted from her own childhood in a City Youth Home.

"There are things in the world our little sisters need to fear, Bren, so we can teach them to defend themselves." Jess stroked Brenna's arm. "Maybe not demons, but there will always be enemies who seek their blood. Our young should learn about them here, in the safety of their mothers' arms. Amazons have never had the luxury of pretending we offer our daughters a sane planet."

Brenna's eyes burned a little from the smoke, and she closed them for a moment. At least half of Tristaine had gathered in the circle of the storyfire, and the comforting presence of other Amazons was proving Jess's point. An assembled clan offered safety.

She looked sleepily from one face to the next as Kyla's melodic voice washed over her. The names came easily to her now, after a year among these women. She made a mental note to tell Dana that she once thought she'd never match histories and faces.

She saw Hakan, who had trained beside Jess under Dyan's tutelage. Hakan sat across the circle holding the hand of her wife, Kas, both of them obviously entranced by Kyla's tale.

Closer to their blanket, Vicar's handsome head rested in the lap of her adonai, Wai Li. Brenna remembered Wai had chosen the name of one of Tristaine's seven founders, a common practice among Amazons. The spirits of those ancient grandmothers lived on in the seven stars of the clan's constellation, just becoming visible overhead now, as the sun faded behind the western ridge.

The first Wai Li had founded Tristaine's guild of mothers, and Brenna smiled at the infant in the arms of Vicar's wife, who slept with the peace of one who knew he'd chosen his parents wisely. Both Vic and Wai Li would probably choose to leave the clan for a period of years when their son entered puberty. He would go with his parents to a rural settlement or a small town open to peaceful neighbors. The City was no longer an option for resettlement, so they would scout the mountain regions for smaller colonies.

"She rises still, when the ghost fog creeps over an Amazon village, blanketing it in silence. Dozens of clans have vanished down the insatiable maw of Botesh," Kyla droned to an utterly silent audience. "She who betrayed her Goddess, she who thirsts for the blood of the adanin, lingers yet. Look for Botesh in the sudden shadows across your path...in the brief chill that sweeps through a fire-warmed lodge, the thick, foul fog swirling fast through a sleeping village..."

Brenna shifted against Jess and picked out Dana's pale features across the fire circle. Her dark eyes were rapt on Kyla's face, in an unguarded moment of longing. Brenna honestly didn't know if Kyla returned Dana's yearning, or was even aware of it. Or much else, besides her grief for Camryn.

Kyla used to sing beautiful songs from Tristaine's past,

Brenna thought. Now she told horror tales of phantom Amazon blood drinkers.

As always when wanting reassurance, Brenna pulled Jess's arms tighter around her and sought out Shann's face. She saw their queen seated gracefully among the older children of the clan, her eyes sparkling as she savored Kyla's tale. In the week of craziness settling on the mesa, there hadn't been time to see much of their lady, and it was good to know she was near.

Brenna felt a small nudge of misgiving. Shann's refined features seemed sallow, even in the rich gold light of the storyfire. There were fine lines bracketing the queen's extraordinary eyes that Brenna had never noticed before, even in times of high crisis. She should waylay Shann when this was over and see if she was on another of her weird ritual fasts.

Jess's breasts pressed against her back, her nipples rising into hard nubs Brenna could feel even through her cloak, and she smiled. In spite of her inherent modesty, Brenna took a certain pride in her ability to arouse Jess at unexpected times. Then Brenna realized Jess was probably responding to the compelling music of Kyla's voice as she reached the climax of her tale.

"Botesh *strikes*," the girl hissed, her auburn hair shimmering in the firelight. "Sharp tongue, sharp talons, sharp fangs, sharp—"

Jess goosed Brenna in the ribs, and she shrieked like a crazed harpy. Heads whipped toward them, and a few of the younger children yelled too, enjoying their fright.

The Amazons snorted laughter into the warm circle. Kyla's look of surprise dissolved, and she grinned and applauded with the others, recognizing the perfect cap to a ghost story when she heard one.

"Spontaneous human combustion." Brenna twisted to glare at Jess, who had one hand plastered over her mouth to stifle her grin. *Another theory disproved*, she thought, and later wrote in her journal, *If people were actually capable of bursting into flames, I would be doing it. And then I would do it to Jesstin.*

❖

As the storyfire was allowed to burn down to embers in the village square, Dana and Hakan walked home with Brenna and Jess. Dana had elected to bunk with the rest of the guild of warriors in one of the larger lodges on the southern rim of the mesa, and the cabin Hakan shared with her mate lay in the forest beyond it.

A white glaze of frost was already beginning to form on the hard-packed dirt path. The mountains at night held a quality of deep silence Brenna had never experienced in the City. The void of sound could be harrowing, comforting, or awe-inducing, depending on her mood, which was pensive at the moment. Jess's arm felt good around her shoulders, as naturally balanced and relaxed there now as an extension of her own body. The pine scents around her were fresh and tantalizing, and her belly was full of a savory broth. The air was fresh and crisp on her face after the warmth of the storyfire. Perhaps it was just Kyla's ghostly tale that kept the nape of Brenna's neck prickling.

"Is this, like, a royal command?" Dana's voice drifted to them. "Shann says I have to be on this high council or, what, I get sold to slavers?"

"Shann requested your presence at our next council. She didn't command it," Hakan corrected. She strolled easily beside Dana, her large hands clasped behind her. "And Tristaine never barters with slave traders. Slaughters them, but never barters."

Brenna smiled. Like Shann, the courteous Hakan always

answered every question thoroughly, regardless of ironic overtones.

Dana had stopped walking and was staring at Hakan's broad back as she continued down the path with Jesstin and Brenna. Then she ran a few steps to catch up.

"Slavers? I was kidding. These mountains have slavers?"

"Shann means to honor you, Dana, by naming you to her council." Jess glanced at her over Brenna's head. "She wants to add a fresh voice from outside our clan. A new perspective."

"And she sees something in you she trusts," Brenna added.

"Sheesh." Dana scowled, slapping at the underbrush with the long stick she carried. "Either you guys...sheesh."

"What?" Brenna prompted before they parted briefly to walk around a towering pine.

"Nothing," Dana grumbled. "Just trying to keep my status straight, here. Either you Amazons trust me too much, like your queen, or no one trusts me at all, like Sirius and everyone else around here. And none of you know me from jack, either way."

"Stop sulking, youngster." Hakan gave Dana's shoulder a friendly tap, which would have spun her face-first into a tree if Brenna hadn't steadied her. "Keep in mind that the first time most of our sistren saw you, you were tasering Jesstin in the gut."

Jess's hand brushed unconsciously across her lower side, and Dana dropped her gaze. Brenna frowned at Hakan and touched Dana's forearm.

"The first time Hakan and Vicar met me," Brenna confided, "I was about to pitch fanny-first off the side of a sheer cliff and take Kyla and Camryn down with me. This will be written up in the annals of Tristaine history as the worst introduction any woman ever made to her sisters. Yours is a close second, though." Brenna smiled. "I'm just saying give it some time, Dana. Settling in can be tough."

Jess caught Dana's eye for a moment and winked. Dana's grin restored her to the handsome young woman she was, and she jogged to catch up with Hakan.

After Hakan and Dana disappeared into the trees, Brenna and Jess angled toward their small cabin, which stood in a thick copse of pines to the right of the path.

Brenna leaned into Jess's warmth. Selene flew in full ghostly glory above them, bathing the quiet woods in cool blue light.

"Shann looks tired, Jesstin."

"She does?" Jess guided her around a snarl of shrubs in the path. "Ah, lass, Shann's got the strength of ten."

"Maybe." Brenna shrugged. "Maybe I just can't remember that Shann's almost fifty, when she looks and moves like she's half that. But she does seem tired these days." She tapped Jess's side. "And so do you, my tough friend."

Jess stopped midyawn and rubbed the back of her neck. "It was a long migration, Bren. Getting this village set up took a lot out of all of us."

"Not really. What did we have to set up? There were almost a hundred empty cabins here, ready for us to just walk into. And a half-dozen bigger lodges to house our guilds. Jesstin, that's another thing."

Brenna hopped in front of Jess, then turned to face her, walking backwards. "This still seems way too perfect to me. I mean, how often does an exiled Amazon clan just stumble onto a ready-made village, way the heck up in the boondocks?"

"It may not be as miraculous as you'd think, lass." Jess grinned and took Brenna's arm, turning her so she could see where they walked. "The City has always bred defectors. Who knows how many little castoff communities have settled in these hills in the last hundred years?"

"But this mesa is old, Jesstin. Shann said this village is much older than the City, and it's definitely Amazon. But even she doesn't recognize those markings all over that creepy altar."

"What's your point, Bren?" Jess's tone had taken on a slight edge, and Brenna blinked up at her.

"I also notice that some of our warriors are growing a wee bit testy." Brenna smiled. "Kyla's seeing it too. She mentioned it the other—"

"You and our little sister Kyla worry too much, young Brenna." A roguish smile touched Jess's lips, and she pressed Brenna back against the smooth trunk of a white aspen. "About our adanin. About a queen's weariness and a toddler's nightmares…"

Brenna's eyebrows quirked through her spiky bangs. "What are we doing?"

"I am reassurin' you, so you will not worry no more." Jess pressed against Brenna's softness and untied the laces that held her cloak closed at her throat.

"Aha. This is why you're tired. Our serial ravishings." Brenna smirked and tapped her fingers lightly. "What is it with you these days, Jesstin? You're insatiable."

"Ye drive me mad with desire, wench." Jess nibbled on Brenna's throat, and her hands began taking liberties, rubbing over the fabric covering the taut mounds of her breasts.

"Jess." Brenna pushed her back. "Hearth and home are only about twenty yards, thataway."

"I want ye here." A familiar growl roughened Jess's low voice, one Brenna usually welcomed in the privacy of their blankets. She liked it less under a tree on a cold night. After ghost stories about evil spirit cannibals. "I'll take ye here and now."

"Well, sorry. Flattered, but sorry." Brenna felt her smile fade as Jess's touch grew harsh. One callused palm snuck into the opening of her shirt and scrubbed across one breast, then squeezed it. "Jess, hey. Stop it."

"You talk too much, City girl." Jess didn't ease Brenna back against the tree; she pushed her against it and ripped her shirt open with one brutal yank.

"Hey! *Jesstin!*" Brenna slapped her, hard. Her palm cracked against the side of her face like a rifle shot, and the force of the blow actually forced Jess back a step.

Jess glared at her, and, for a moment, a frightening tinge of silver entered her eyes. Then the silver light faded, and she was Jess again.

"*What?* Crikey, you have my attention." Jess rubbed the side of her face, scowling. Then she blinked and stared at Brenna. "You all right, Bren? You're half-naked out here in front of Gaia and everyone! Did I do that?"

"Yeah." Brenna tied her shirt closed, her heart hammering. "Are you all right? Tell me how you feel, Jess."

"Cold," Jess answered promptly. She took a step and rubbed Brenna's arms briskly, and this time the strength in those hands comforted, as it always had. "You're shaking, Bren."

"Of course I'm shaking. You've never touched me like that before." She stilled Jess's hands and studied her face. "You really don't remember, do you?"

"What's to remember? Kyla's tale has you seeing ghosts, lass." Jess slid an arm around Brenna's waist. "Let's get you home and warm, querida. I'll not bed an icicle tonight, no matter how cute."

Brenna cast one last look over her shoulder toward the village square. The rings of trees that separated their cabin from the storyfire pit were spaced, with odd perfection, to allow a clear view of the altar in its center.

She shivered again and tightened her arm around Jess.

CHAPTER THREE

Far from her Celtic homeland
She sleeps bereft of hope
Goddess grant her peace

Brenna studied the odd inscription on the gravestone as Hakan read the words aloud. She was grateful for Hakan's solid warmth on her left and Kyla's on her right. The wind on this desolate hill blew in cold, fitful gusts. Winter was coming, Brenna remembered, and graveyards made such random thoughts feel ominous.

Tristaine's scouting party had come across the old cemetery just as the sun crested midday. The large yard, encircled by a low rock fence, lay almost a full league from their mesa, on a barren slope deep in the forest. Flat oval stones of every shape and size canted at angles all over the burial ground. Every grave held an epitaph and, apparently, the earthly remains of an Amazon warrior.

"I thought Amazons preferred cremation." Brenna studied the variety of glyphs etched in the markers and folded her arms against a chill breeze.

"Tristaine does, most of us." Hakan's hands were clasped behind her back, a respectful stance. "But several of these stones bear the language of my country and the dialect of its Eastern clans. Their customs are different. At any rate, sisters, it's sacred ground."

"With strange and sacred flowers," Brenna murmured. She knelt and studied the small plants that adorned several of the surrounding graves. They held spiked leaves and glossy gold berries, and she'd seen nothing like them in Tristaine's new village.

She almost reached out to pull one free of the hard-packed earth, wanting to see what Shann made of the species and whether they could test it for medicinal qualities. Brenna paused, then lowered her hand as she got to her feet. Tearing a plant's roots from a burial mound felt wrong to her, a violation of the dead warrior's rest.

"But what's a graveyard doing out here, this far from the mesa?" Kyla glanced at one of the oval markers, half-submerged in the marshy earth, and shuddered. She took a sidling step and brushed her arm against Brenna, who lifted hers around Kyla's shoulders with the ease of long practice. "These are the graves of the clan that built our village, right?"

"I guess they have to be," Brenna agreed. "There couldn't have been that many Amazon clans running around out here." She felt Kyla shiver against her and strengthened her protective hold. Kyla had only begun turning to her for comfort again recently, and Brenna welcomed the contact.

There had been an easy warmth between them from the beginning. Unlike Brenna's bond with Camryn, which had taken time to run deep, she had loved Dyan's young blood sister almost at once. Of course, that wasn't a fair comparison. Minutes after Camryn met Brenna, she had decked her with a roundhouse right.

Brenna smiled sadly at the gravestone and rubbed Kyla's arm to warm them both. With the innate protective courtesy of Tristaine's warriors, Hakan took Brenna's and Kyla's hands as they made their way carefully among the worn stones. Brenna noted that the placement of the graves was not random. They formed vaguely circular patterns, much like the rings of trees surrounding their mesa.

Almost every grave held an epitaph, but Brenna saw no numbers that might mean dates on any of them. Oddly, all of the stones seemed equally weathered, as if this desolate cemetery contained the dead of one dreadful mass burial, a hundred warriors all laid to rest the same long-ago day.

What kind of enemy could wipe out an entire Amazon army in one battle, Brenna wondered, leaving a paltry few to bury their sisters, before scattering to the winds themselves? She heard the distant twang of a bowstring as they stepped through the last rows of graves.

"A fine cleavin' of yonder tree, Dana." There was amusement in Jess's voice, and Brenna turned to see her squinting at Dana's arrow, which still vibrated in the trunk of an aspen twenty steps away. Vicar and Jess were conducting archery practice during this break, and Dana was always eager for training.

"You're trying too hard to breathe through the release, adanin." Jess stepped behind Dana to adjust her grip on the red-oak bow. "Relax and let the arrow leave its rest as naturally as the air leaves your lungs."

Brenna loved Jess's voice under any circumstances, but especially at times like this, when she was teaching. That low, friendly, patient tone had introduced her to a dozen new skills—and coaxed her awake from many a nightmare.

Dana was scowling, looking from the arrow in the aspen to the dead stump to its right, her intended target. She set another feathered shaft to her bowline as Jess went to retrieve the first.

"See to it we don't have to memorialize that aspen there, youngster." Vicar was chewing on a long piece of grass, and her tone held its usual ironic edge. "Amazons honor trees. Don't go skewering that one again."

"I've loved trees since I was a kid," Dana grumbled. "Lots of people love trees in the City. We just don't have many of them. You don't have to be an Amazon to love trees."

Brenna realized her palm was sticky with pinesap, and she scowled, wiping it on her jeans. "Sometimes it helps, though."

"But an Amazon would never *murder* a tree, Dana," Kyla called. "The sharp end of that thing points *toward* the stump now."

Brenna would have given her younger sister a nudge to remind her of her manners, but suddenly her head was full of the terrible screaming of stallions in mortal combat. She clenched her hand, still sticky with sap.

"I know which end points toward the stump," Dana sighed. "Come on, a little credit. I've had three years of military train—"

Dana's breath was forcefully punched from her lungs as Vicar lunged and shoved her hard enough to knock her off her feet. Brenna heard the impact of Vicar's palms on Dana's shoulders, which was almost as loud as her crash to the rocky ground, the bow and its arrow falling harmlessly with her. Jess whirled.

"*Vicar*! Sweet Artemis!" Kyla cried as Vic swung one booted foot over Dana's waist and straddled her, her hand on the dagger in her belt. "What's the matter with you?"

"Never point a drawn bow at a woman, idiot, unless you intend to kill!" Vicar's fair face was flushed with anger.

Dana blinked up at her, obviously trying to pull enough breath into her lungs to respond.

"Vicar, back off," Jess barked, tossing the first arrow aside. "Her bow was at rest."

Vic's eyes flashed. "You determined to give her another crack at you, Jesstin?"

The battling stallions bugled fury in Brenna's mind, sending a bolt of pain through her head.

"Hakan, wait," Kyla yelled just as Hakan began a

graceful running dive and plowed bodily into Vicar, knocking her off Dana.

What began badly quickly grew worse.

"I'm tired of your bullying, Vicar," Hakan snarled. The soft mahogany of her eyes had gone muddy with malevolence. She and Vicar both jumped to their feet and began circling each other in a controlled but deadly dance.

Their expressions stunned Brenna, who still stood frozen, the screaming stallions an ongoing roar only she could hear. Kyla ran down the small rise to Dana and helped her up.

"Bloody *pendejas*!" Jess jumped between her two warriors, and Brenna unfroze and darted down the rise.

"No, adanin!" Luckily, Kyla was both alert and nimble. She caught Brenna's arm as she ran by and held on to it. "It's dangerous down there. Let Jess handle this!"

"You go too easy on your cousin, Jesstin. You always have," Hakan spat. "Dyan would never abide this woman's—"

"That's enough, Hakan," Jess snapped.

"Don't invoke Dyan, Hakan. I knew her far better!" Vicar's handsome features radiated hatred, her long fingers stiff and clawed. "Why do you defend this young City bitch, Jess? She almost killed you!"

Jess's mouth opened, but then Hakan dived again, so Jess did too. She caught Hakan in midair and threw her back. The big warrior's arms pinwheeled madly as she staggered on the rocky ground, her braids whipping around her head, but she kept her footing.

Jess turned and very nearly caught Vicar's forearm in the throat as she bolted past her. One hand snuck out and caught a handful of blond hair, and Jess, snarling, hauled her taller cousin back.

It became a brutal dance. Hakan charged at Vicar, and Jess intercepted her and shoved her back. Then Vicar attacked

Hakan, and Jess pivoted, caught her, and threw her in the other direction. Then Hakan charged again.

Brenna was about to do anything in her power to get Kyla to let go of her arm. She would regret it later if she bruised Kyla, she really would, but if she wasn't allowed to get to Jess—

"Whoa, *whoa!*" Brenna lunged as Dana started past her, apparently having similar thoughts. She caught Dana around the waist and held on, yelling for Kyla. Introducing Dana to the combustible trio below now would be disastrous.

"Dana, you stay *here!*" Kyla's voice could fill Tristaine's village square, and now it rang quite clearly amid the restless dead around them. "What *is* it with you City women, Brenna? You have *no* common sense at first, *zero*, none!"

Now Vicar and Hakan were nose to nose, or would have been, were Jess not sandwiched between them, and Jess roared, "In Dyan's name!"

Abruptly, finally, it all started to pass—the rage of the warriors and the screaming of horses in Brenna's mind.

Hakan and Vicar stood motionless, still in defensive stance. No one had drawn any weapons, but that was no comfort to Brenna. All three Amazons were capable of killing with their hands.

"Stand down," Jess panted, and they did. Vicar and Hakan both straightened and stared at each other. That frightening light had left their faces, leaving only the flush of exertion and cold.

Jess braced her hands on her knees, still watching her two warriors carefully, taking deep, even breaths, her breath pluming out in clouds of steam. "Someone tell me," she growled, "what the bloody hell that was all about."

"She raised her bow, Jesstin." Vicar's tone was subdued.

"She did not." Jess straightened slowly. "Hear me, Vicar.

Dana's shaft was down. I saw it. Dana?" She turned toward Brenna and the others, who waited up the small rise. "Speak for yourself, girl."

"Yeah, Jess." Dana's voice was strained, and she cleared her throat. "My arrow was down, and the bowstring was lax."

Vic rested her hands on her hips and spat at the rocky ground, but her downcast eyes now looked more troubled than defiant.

"I've never seen you go off like that, Hakan." Kyla's voice was a bit unsteady. "This big blond bully with the brogue, I can understand, but *you*?" She went to Vicar and took her hand without fear, patting it in loving reproach.

Vicar sighed. Kyla was one of the protected few who never felt the bite of her temper. "Aye, little sister. You're right. My blood runs too hot sometimes, and I make an ass of myself. I know it." She regarded Dana evenly and extended her hand.

Dana accepted Vicar's apology, clasping her corded wrist, but her eyes were still wary.

Some of the tension melted out of Brenna's spine as she scratched a small circle between Jess's shoulders.

Vicar caught Hakan's eye, and Brenna saw a dozen communications fly silently between them.

"I forgot Dyan's teaching," Vic said at last. In Tristaine, there was no more eloquent admission of fault and human frailty.

Hakan nodded, and warmth crept back into her dark eyes.

Brenna swallowed and heard a dry click in her throat. That nerve-fraying sound of battling horses had faded but still lingered, a sibilant horror in her inner ear. Brenna moved into the circle, peering closely at Hakan, then Vicar. She took Vicar's pulse at the wrist. "Do you feel anything strange, Vic?"

"Aye, my cousin's adonai is coming on to me. That is strange," Vicar droned.

Jess's lip curled, which relieved some of the residual tension.

"Otherwise, nay, lass."

"These cretins were too clumsy to do any real damage, Bren." Jess clawed her wild hair out of her eyes, then checked the passage of the sun. "Let's head back by way of the river. It's a sunny ride. I've had more than enough grim shadows for the day."

"I'm with you." Dana sighed.

They gathered their weapons and headed for the stand of trees where their horses stood, ground-tied.

Brenna snuck her arm through Jess's as they passed the last of the gravestones, the sparse pines overhead sighing in farewell. None of them looked back.

❖

"This is humiliating, I've decided." Brenna's face was warm now against Jess's denim-clad back. She rode behind her on Bracken. "Sticking to your back like lint on a sock. Teach me to ride, Jesstin."

"You're serious, querida?" Jess's hair swept across Brenna's face as she turned her head. "I'd be most pleased."

"I have to learn to ride. Mountain Amazons ride horses." Brenna stated the fact much as she would a medical reality, like "teeth decay."

She loved horses, especially Bracken—and Valkyrie, that huge, beautiful beast of Hakan's. But she also maintained that even Jess's strong little mustang, the shrimp of the herd, was far too high off the ground.

She watched their shadow move like a two-headed centaur over the sunlit trunks of the trees they passed, followed by their four sisters on their own mounts. Now that the strange Amazon burial ground was well behind them, the weak sun stood a better chance of banishing the chill.

Brenna surveyed the passing scenery, glorious in late autumn, and remembered the journal entry she had made last night.

If the people of the City could see the real beauty of these mountains, Caster and her Governmental ilk would stand no chance of holding them behind electrified walls. No wonder art and poetry featuring nature are so regulated there. And travel has always been fiercely restricted in every City, along with most other freedoms that threaten Homeland Security.

The Amazons rode a natural path that flanked the eastern side of a broad river that ran west, about a quarter league from their mesa. Its roaring currents were stoked by a summer of melting glaciers higher in the hills. Their path back to the mesa followed it closely, but rose and dipped to fit the contours of the hillside. Jess was right. It made for a beautiful ride. They had never explored this far downstream.

Jess's callused fingers warmed the back of Brenna's hand. "You're still cold, Bren."

"I know." Brenna tightened her hold on Jess's waist. "The graves got to me, I think. All those lost warriors. Then Vicar jumping Dana—and, worse, Hakan going after Vic. Did you see their faces, Jesstin?"

"I did." Jess glanced back up the trail to check their privacy. Their four sisters rode together several yards behind Bracken. "That's twice Vicar's gone odd on us since we found this mesa."

"Vicar's not alone," Brenna pointed out.

"Aye, I'm not forgetting Sirius."

"It's hitting you too, Jesstin. Whatever it is. You really scared me the other night."

Jess's shoulders tensed. "Brenna, for the life of me, I don't remember—"

"I'm hearing the stallions again, Jess."

Jess turned her head sharply, and Bracken whickered at

the sudden movement. "You heard them today?"

Brenna nodded and shivered. "Fighting to the death. It started just before Vicar went at Dana."

She let Jess absorb this unwelcome news. In the past, visions of horses had warned Brenna of real dangers threatening Tristaine. As portents, they were grimly reliable, but maddeningly vague. After a moment, Jess let out a long breath.

"All right, Bren. We've got too many questions to answer alone. Gaia knows we have reason to abide by your instincts. Shann's high council meets tonight. We'll talk to our lady about these concerns before our sisters gather."

Brenna kissed the back of Jess's shoulder, then rested her head against her again and closed her eyes. Jess's warmth was banishing the last of her chills, and she relaxed into Bracken's steady, rocking gait. She heard Kyla's light tone as the other riders caught up to them.

"Dana, you're still mixing up your terms. You should have had all this down months ago." Kyla clicked to her horse, and he caught up to Bracken. "Remember, Blades? The first day we met, I taught you the difference between adanin and adonai."

"Yes, I seem to remember that." Warmth rose in Brenna as she savored the memory.

"When was this, now?" Jess asked, speaking loudly as they rode near the river's fast, noisy current.

"It was after the four of us escaped from the Clinic." Brenna patted Jess's stomach. "But before Shann found us in the foothills. You told Kyla and Camryn that I was your adanin, so they had to accept me, too."

"It was a struggle," Kyla added, "but we managed it."

"You two were incorrigible," Jess grumbled. "I've never seen such a capacity for *talk*. A flood o' words! Camryn and I thought we were going to have to drug you both just to save our sanity."

"Really? To save yer sanity, missy?" Kyla mocked Jess's brogue in dead-on imitation. "And you'd drug us both, eh? You and Camryn and what army, Jesstin?"

Brenna felt a touch of relief. Kyla had spoken the name of her dead wife naturally, for the first time in recent memory. And the gradual return of her banter with Jess was encouraging as well. Shann said the bond Jesstin and Kyla shared could not be severed by anything short of a chainsaw, and Brenna believed it.

"Hold up." Jess touched her mustang's neck, and their column halted.

"Is that a bridge?" Dana lifted a hand to shade her eyes and pointed at the neat split-log structure spanning the wide river up ahead on their left. "Well. Duh. I know it's a bridge, but who built it?"

"More to the point, who's on it?" Jess murmured, and Brenna craned past her to look.

It took a moment to see what Jess's sharp eyes had detected. A slender figure stood in the center of the bridge, arms resting on the waist-high railing, facing downriver, away from them. It clearly wasn't one of their sisters. Gender was impossible to determine at this distance, and the figure stood so still it didn't seem alive until a breeze generated by the churning waters lifted a scrap of light brown hair.

Brenna tried to quell her first instinct that was, as always, to scream to her sisters, "Run!" A stranger in their midst didn't have to mean disaster, but whoever this person was, there were questions to answer.

"Vicar, Hakan." Jess lifted one long leg over Bracken's neck and dropped lightly to the ground. "I see no weapons. No need to scare him, or her. But let's go make our introductions."

"Aye, Jess." Vicar and Hakan dismounted, and the three women took a moment to check their arms.

Brenna chewed her lower lip. She hated suspense. She kept her eyes trained on the distant figure. There was no menace or distress evident in the stranger's posture. Brenna could see white hands on the log railing, and the shoulders—slender, probably female—looked relaxed.

J'heika, rise.

"Uh oh," Brenna whispered.

Jess looked up at her curiously.

Ride, Brenna, now! You've no time!

She felt a moment of panic. It was obvious no one else was hearing this imperious command. *Me, ride?*

Save the girl, or she'll destroy herself!

"Brenna?" Jess squinted at her, frowning.

Brenna heard the concern in Jess's tone, and she would have answered her, but suddenly, in one smooth motion, the figure on the bridge leaped over the railing. There was a final flick of light hair, then a small splash over the roiling din of the current.

Jess cursed, Kyla gasped, then things happened very quickly.

Hakan and Vicar broke into a run for the bridge.

The voice roared, *Brenna! Ride!* Brenna scooted forward, grabbed the horse's reins, and kicked him as hard as she could and still be sure she wouldn't hurt his furry sides. Bracken wasn't used to Brenna's touch on his neck, but he knew the friendly feel of her legs, and he shot down the trail like a guided missile on the hoof.

"Brenna!" Jess bellowed behind her. "Get back here!"

Under certain circumstances, Brenna acknowledged, as she clung to Bracken's plunging neck, certain people might argue that Jess had just given her a direct order. But she had no time to explain herself—or, rather, explain that an invisible banshee with a brogue was ordering her around—so she had to believe that Jess would just trust her and come quickly to save her butt, because Brenna had all she could do to stay on Bracken's back and out of the river.

Then that malted burr sounded in her mind again. *Can you swim?*

Which actually made Brenna a little mad as well as terrified as she and the mustang thundered closer to the log bridge. *Why does everyone,* she thought, *even mysterious voices, always assume that all women from the City are puny and hopeless?*

My own adonai was City-born, ye daft girl, and so was that poor bairn up there, but neither of them can swim! Can you swim?

"I'm an *athlete.* Of course I can *swim!*" Brenna yelled.

Don't speak astride, in full gallop, young idjit. You'll break yer teeth! There's the girl, see her?

Brenna summoned her courage and lifted her head to peer between Bracken's large ears as they galloped past the bridge and continued downstream. The wind of their passage swept her hair into her eyes. Blinded by the sun sparking off the swirling rapids, for a terrible moment, she *didn't* see her. And then she did. Her close-cropped head was bobbing above the surface of the deep water in the middle of the swift-moving river. "Yeah, she's there!"

Jump!

"What?"

Great crikey, how will we face what's coming if you can't follow simple orders? Now, jump!

"Into the *river?*"

Are you deaf as well as mouthy? I said jump!

So Brenna did.

She didn't think; she just gathered herself on Bracken's sturdy back, drew a deep breath, and hurled herself up and sideways over the bushes lining the steep bank of the river and smack into the water, blue as Jess's eyes and colder than Caster's heart.

It closed over her head. The shock of chill punched the air out of her lungs, and for a sick instant Brenna flailed helplessly in the current, head over heels. Then instinct caught up with her, and she began to move with the force of the water rather than resist it.

Sight the girl. Keep your eyes on her. Jesstin's coming.

She had no time to look over her shoulder to see Jess thundering along the side of the river on Hakan's huge horse, but knew with certainty that is what she would see. She also realized that, at full gallop, he ran faster than the current, but the river had a lead on him and Jess, pulling both Brenna and the woman inexorably westward.

Brenna finally sighted the drowning woman. *Thank Artemis, there she is*, she thought, *or thank Gaia, or whatever goddess an Amazon should invoke while trying to rescue a stranger from a suicide attempt.* She could see pale, thin arms flail and hear the woman's weak gasping as she drew near her.

Finally, Brenna snagged her heavy, waterlogged cloak.

"Leave me alone!"

It was a ragged cry, and Brenna ignored it. She let an eddy of water surge her against the flailing figure and wrapped one arm around her tightly from behind.

"Shut up!" Brenna gasped. "I'm saving your life! Hold on! Help's—" she choked on a throatful of melted glacier. "Help's coming!"

"Brenna!"

Apparently if Jess was also hearing a spectral voice telling her not to talk while at full gallop, she was ignoring it, too. Brenna chanced a quick glance over her shoulder as she spun with the small woman in her arms and saw a flash of dark hair as Jess stood on Valkyrie's back and dived over the embankment into the river. Brenna almost gave herself whiplash trying to track her fall, and her already hammering heart gave a nasty lurch until she saw Jess's head burst through the swirling water.

Jess's strong arms pulled her to them in seconds, and she grabbed the woman's trailing leg. She barked at Brenna, "You all right?"

Brenna's energy was fading fast, so she just nodded, and they began the arduous trek to the shallows of the riverside, swimming hard against the current. The woman lay limp and unresisting between them. Her cloak covered much of her face, but her parted lips were blue. The sight of them scared Brenna, and she kicked hard in the water to stay in place and felt for a pulse. It was there, faint, but fast and steady.

They reached the embankment and were pulling the slight form out of the water when they heard the sound of horses. Vicar and Hakan jumped off Vic's roan on the path above as Dana and Kyla trotted up on their own mounts, leading Bracken.

"Dead?" Vic called, sidestepping down the bank to receive the unconscious girl from Jess's arms.

"No, but check her breathing," Brenna gasped. She let herself slump to the grassy bank, suddenly and completely spent.

Then she was suddenly and completely lying on her back, her hands on either side of her head, and Jess was kneeling over her, her eyes inches from her own.

"Explanation," Jess barked.

"Let me breathe first," Brenna got out, and Jess relented and gave her time. The tenderness in her touch as she brushed Brenna's wet hair off her forehead belied the sternness in her voice.

"How is she, Jess?"

Jess raised her eyes to the path. "Vicar?"

"The girl's sound enough, Jesstin!" Brenna heard Vicar call from above. "She's coming around. You two okay?"

"Peachy," Jess shot back, and glared down at Brenna. "Well? You ignored my direct command. You may not be pledged to the guild of warriors, lass, but *no* Amazon can—"

"Unless guided by greater access to information," Brenna panted. She squinted up against the weak sun to see her lover. "I heard another voice, Jess."

"Oh." The anger drained out of Jess's face. "Whose?"

"Jesstin, Brenna, you'd best come!" Hakan was looking down at them, her hands on her knees. "This bairn says she knows you! She escaped from the City Prison."

Brenna and Jess exchanged a stunned glance, then moved as quickly up the embankment as their stiff legs would allow.

The young woman was wrapped in a blanket, reclining in Dana's arms as Kyla massaged her thin legs. This simple Amazon technique for treating shock was more effective than any chemical intervention. The girl's hair was damp and stringy against her pale forehead, and her eyes were closed.

Jess knelt beside her and lifted her hand. "My name is Jesstin, lass. You're safe with us. No one here will hurt you. I promise."

The girl's eyes fluttered open, and she gazed at Jess. "Not you." She shivered, hard. "I don't know you." The green eyes sought out Brenna's face. "There you are."

Brenna's heart stopped. "Sammy," she whispered.

CHAPTER FOUR

Hello, Samantha." Her smile friendly and warm, Shann glanced over her shoulder at Brenna. "I believe she's back with us, Blades."

Brenna tossed the cloth she'd been drying her hands with and went to the bedside. Shann made room for her, and Brenna sat carefully on the bunk's edge, noting how Samantha's shadowed eyes tracked her movements.

"Hey, you. Try to stay awake." Brenna lifted her sister's cold hand onto her knee and took her pulse at the wrist. The beat was slower, more even, not the fast, feathery pace that had alarmed them earlier. Brenna frowned, concerned by the glassiness of Sammy's stare. "Sam, you know me, right?"

It took Samantha a few moments to reply. "Yes, sure, Bree."

Brenna found a tremulous smile when she heard the old nickname, but it faded fast. Samantha's voice was hoarse, and she looked much older than her twenty-one years. In the eighteen months since Brenna had seen her, she had dropped a good twenty pounds. Her eyes were bracketed by lines, and her fair skin seemed stretched across the delicate bones of her face. Her complexion held an unhealthy, waxy pallor. The vibrant red-gold of Sammy's hair, her glory in childhood, had faded to a lank brown, cut short against her neck. Brenna let her hand hover over Sammy's flat waist, then settle on the fur covering her.

"You're in a safe place, Sammy." She brushed small circles over Samantha's stomach. "We were worried about hypothermia, but you seem to be coming around just—"

"They took the baby. She died."

Brenna stilled her hand. "What?" she whispered.

"The baby," Samantha repeated. Her unwavering gaze was fixed on Brenna's face. "I only saw her once. She was born in Prison."

"Sam." Brenna clenched her sister's hand.

"And Matt's dead, Bree."

"Ah, no." Brenna hunched her shoulders beneath these blows. She didn't know which was worse, the news of Samantha's terrible loss, or her utter lack of expression as she reported it.

Brenna felt a light touch on her head and looked up to meet Shann's compassionate gaze. "Matthew was my sister's adonai, lady," she explained softly. "Tell me what happened, Sam."

"Caster happened." Samantha closed her eyes and settled more deeply into the softness of the furs beneath her. "Water?"

Shann's hand rested on Samantha's hair. "We can do better than that." She fit a cup of steaming liquid into Brenna's numb fingers.

"Careful, it's hot." Brenna held the tea to her sister's chapped lips and supported her neck while she sipped it. Sammy seemed to need rest after this brief exchange, and Brenna was grateful for the silence.

The story emerged in fits and starts. Brenna had already grasped the sickening highlights. After she and Jess had escaped from the Clinic, Caster couldn't believe Brenna hadn't told her only blood relative about the plan.

"I couldn't believe it either," Samantha said.

She had been arrested on a conspiracy charge. Her

husband, Matthew, died in a fiery car accident trying to evade Caster's pursuing agents.

Samantha's baby was born in the Prison infirmary. She had held the infant only once before it was taken. Sammy was told she died days later.

"I got to tell her that her name was Brenna," Samantha finished. "Matt and I agreed to that as soon as we knew she was coming. We didn't get a chance to tell you before you disappeared."

"Sammy." Brenna's throat was painfully tight. "I'm so sorry."

"You could have warned us." Samantha's tone was mild.

"Sam, honestly, there was no time—"

"It doesn't matter now." Samantha's eyes were drifting closed again, but she forced them open, and for the first time they carried a spark of feeling. "Bree?"

"Yes."

"I'm glad you're okay. I was scared for you."

"I love you so much, kid."

Samantha nodded against the pillow, her voice fading, "...love you back."

❖

Brenna stepped outside the cabin that served as Tristaine's healing lodge and leaned against one of the oak posts supporting its deck. She rested her forehead on her crossed hands, the relief of tears after such long restraint as welcome as a warm bath.

Brenna had always wept silently, a trait she shared with Jess. Even as a child, during the years she and Samantha shared a narrow cot in the County Youth Home, her grief had been voiceless. The comfort Brenna longed for then never came, but now it was here. She heard the cabin door open behind her, then felt Shann's hand, gentle and strong on her shoulder.

Brenna knew Shann understood that grief tended to close women's throats, and she wouldn't expect Brenna to talk. Shann stood beside her, her arm around her waist, letting her regal presence lend the kind of loving support mere words couldn't hope to convey.

After a while, Brenna was able to raise her head from her hands and draw a few hitching breaths. "She's still sleeping?"

"Yes, the valerian tea worked well." Shann stroked Brenna's hair. "Your Sammy should rest comfortably until morning. Vicar and Wai Li will watch over her during our night's council. With care and time, Blades, she'll recover physically."

Shann reached into an inner pocket of her robe and pulled out a small, plastic-wrapped package. "I found this in your blood sister's shirt, adanin. Samantha protected it well."

Brenna opened the plastic and stared at the tattered notebook inside. "Shann. It's my first journal."

Shann nodded. "You must have found an excellent hiding place for it."

"You told me to leave it behind last spring, wrapped in a tree, safe from the flood. With directions to our first camp." Brenna brushed the back of her hand across her eyes. "And you ordered maps placed at each of our camps as we traveled, lady. Sammy never would have found us otherwise. How can I thank you for that?"

Shann opened her arms, and Brenna went into them willingly, her head fitting neatly beneath Shann's chin. She rested against her elder sister for a moment.

"Sammy named her baby for me." Brenna found herself empty of tears, which was good, or repeating that memory would have closed her throat for another hour. She filled her lungs with cold mountain air, then breathed it out and tried to focus on Shann's voice.

"Brenna, I must ask you to call upon all your courage now. You must face your grief head-on. We have grave work to do, and it begins tonight. I'm going to need your help."

"With what?"

"Listen first. Samantha is alive." Shann's smile was radiant. "Brenna, your little sister lives! You haven't even had time to digest that one lovely grace before you were hit with sorrows."

"You're right, lady," Brenna whispered. She lifted her shoulders a little as she registered her surroundings again. The sun was setting over the forested western slopes, but it wasn't terribly cold yet. An early, full moon ghosted her way up the sky.

"Lady...Brenna?"

Jess was walking toward the cabin's deck, a sight so healing to Brenna's sore heart her knees almost buckled. Jess's eyes were shadowed with concern as she lifted Brenna's cold hands and warmed them in her own.

"How do you feel, adonai?" Jess's low brogue was tender.

Brenna considered. "I'm tired. I'm hungry. Sore. I still have water in my left ear." She sank into Jess's arms and hugged her fiercely. "And *Sammy's alive,* Jesstin."

"She is, lass. We have new family to celebrate tonight." She met Shann's fond gaze over Brenna's shoulder. "Your council gathers, lady."

"Hm." Shann's eyebrow lifted. "And has Aria arrived yet?"

"She has, Shann." Jess grinned. "Aria and her sixty skillets of dinner await us in the square."

"Well, we'll not keep them waiting." Shann took Jess's arm and Brenna's, and they started down the tree-lined path leading into the village.

Tristaine was unusually quiet in the gathering dusk.

Brenna saw other Amazons filtering through the trees in pairs and small groups, finishing the day's work or heading home to their lodges. A few called greetings, which Jess returned with a lifted hand.

Brenna drew in a breath of fresh air, savoring its scent. Faint tendrils of woody smoke reached her from cooking fires, blending with the spicy pine and rich loam of the surrounding forest. Those aromas evoked a feeling of home and safety for Brenna more potent than any sight could. But there was something strange about the camp's stillness.

She heard no laughter among the women they passed. Their voices were hushed and their greetings subdued. And there was no music. Tristaine was a clan that had always cherished song, and many Amazons carried small instruments with them. The air was usually full of soft, separate melodies. Not this night.

"Do you hear it, Blades?" Shann asked.

"I don't hear much, lady. That worries me."

"Exactly." Shann sighed, her gray eyes moving over the lodges that housed her Amazons. "This numb silence has lasted for days now. Brenna told me about the concerns the two of you share, Jesstin, while we sat with Samantha. Of all the signs we're seeing, I think it's the loss of our laughter that chills me most."

Brenna heard a faint grinding sound. Looking over at Jess, she saw the muscles in her jaw stand out. Shann nudged her lead warrior.

"What troubles you, Jess?"

Jess shook her hair out of her eyes, scanning the trees around them. "Nothing new, lady. Or nothing specific. I just don't like enemies I can't see."

"Ah." Shann patted Brenna's hand. "It's especially hard on our warriors, Brenna, these vague portents. Ephemeral threats can't be fought with steel. Strange hostilities between

Amazons who are bound as adanin...a creeping malaise that weighs down our spirits."

"Warriors who get spit sideways off their horses," Brenna added.

"Yes, poor Vicar. It started there."

"And those stallions, and the voice you heard today, Bren." Jess's hand went to the dagger in her belt, an unconscious protective gesture. "It said something was coming. The ghostie didn't offer anything more helpful?"

"You know everything I do." Brenna paused as Jess maneuvered her and Shann carefully around a root embedded in their path. "This voice was different from those I've heard before. Very pushy, might I add. But it helped us save Sam..."

Brenna's voice drifted off and she stopped, peering at Shann in the ebbing light that revealed the shadows beneath her eyes and the sallow dryness of her skin. "Shann—hey. You're not feeling any better, are you?"

"Not a bit," Shann admitted.

"You're sick, lady?" Jess's brow creased, and she touched her dagger again. "How bad is it?"

"Jess, I told you she was looking tired weeks ago." Brenna's impatience was all for herself. Studying Shann now, she was appalled she hadn't addressed her health sooner.

"Relax, girls." The corner of Shann's mouth lifted. "I'm touched, but fatigue is about the worst of it. I'll catch up on my rest once we get a grip on what's plaguing our clan. Come on. I smell a roasted boar out there with my crest on it."

"I want to examine you after the council, Shann." Brenna kept her hand on Shann's arm. "No excuses. You really don't look good to me."

"I'll thank you for it, Blades." Shann smiled. "This is a bad time for Tristaine to suffer a weakened queen." Jess met Brenna's worried gaze and kept a supportive hand on the small of Shann's back as they entered the village square.

The council that advised Tristaine's queen had changed in the last year. The Amazons still mourned the deaths of Jocelyn and Dorothea, two of their elder members, taken by fever within days of each other. Shann's selection of Dana to her inner circle was not greeted with universal joy. She had met privately with several women angered by the City soldier's inclusion.

In addition to Dana, Kyla had been named to the council to represent the clan's youth, a position Camryn had held before a crossbow bolt took her life. Brenna saw her standing near a bank of tables laden with fragrant platters of food.

Kyla seemed to feel her gaze, and her eyes lit when she spotted Brenna. She trotted over to the three women, nodding respectfully to Shann before taking Brenna's hands.

"How is she, sweetie? Your sister?"

"She'll mend, Ky, thanks." Brenna smiled. "I can't wait for you two to know each other. You've always reminded me a bit of Sammy. You're both cheeky as hell."

"Hey, I already know she's from excellent stock." Kyla gave Brenna a quick kiss on the cheek, then stepped back and regarded her and Jess sternly. "Lady? Would you please command these two idiots here to wear life jackets wherever they go now? You should have seen them pitch head over fanny into that river! I almost bit my tongue in half."

"I'm just as glad Gaia spared me that sight." Shann brushed Kyla's hair off her brow. "And grateful you spared your tongue, adanin. We'll need your voice tonight."

"...and I will cheerfully tweak your colon with a fork, barbarian, if you *dare* refer to this sumptuous feast again as *grub*!"

They turned to watch the third new councilor, a voluptuous blond woman named Aria, as she wrapped steely fingers around Dana's neck and escorted her on a forcible survey of the food laid out before them.

"What you slandered as *pork chops* is, in actuality, a savory and tender wild boar, slow-roasted with garlic and fresh herbs. Served with a reduction of wild berries, green onions, and the finest elderberry wine in Tristaine."

"It looks great," Dana stammered, obviously trying not to grin as Aria led her to the next platter. "Everything smells fantastic. Really. I meant to compliment—"

"*And* these are not *spuds,* churl. These are indigenous *rrrr*oot vegetables caramelized slowly, *slowly* and to perfection, and seasoned with pork fat." Aria hit that last "t" with great precision.

"Your problem child's in trouble again," Jess told Shann, amused. "Young Dana's developed a fine talent for rubbing her sisters raw."

Shann nodded. "Stand by. This might call for someone brawnier than me. *Aria,*" the queen trilled, "what a delightful feast you've conjured for the delectation of our council!"

"*Shanendra!*" Aria released Dana's neck and sashayed to Shann in a swirl of silk robes, pecking her affectionately on both cheeks. "Finally, a royal palate *deserving* of my unrivaled culinary talents. Hello, dear Brenna, and *hello*, you muscle-bound stud muffin!"

Aria raised high on her toes, wound her arms around Jess's neck, and gave her a prolonged, sucking kiss full on the lips.

Brenna smiled politely. For the entire time. She refused to look at Shann or Kyla, who undoubtedly enjoyed watching her expression whenever Jess encountered Aria.

She was actually getting used to this behavior, for the most part. Brenna thought Aria was a complete treasure, and she accepted the fact that the woman was simply incapable, at a cellular level, of chastity in any form. She was Shann's age, and when she was eighty, Aria would still be sexually irresistible to any butch with half a pulse on the planet.

Finally Aria's lips detached from Jess's with a wet pop that echoed through the trees like a faint thunderclap. Jess grinned down at her curvaceous elder and gave her an appreciative wink.

"Yech. Brazen strumpets." Sarah was the oldest Amazon on the council. The moonlight gleamed off her bald scalp. Her voice was harsh and cracked—not so much from age, as from the pipe always clenched between her teeth. Her dark eyes were shrouded in a fine web of wrinkles, but they glittered with a sharp intelligence that had guided Shann well. Brenna loved and honored Sarah and tried devoutly to avoid her notorious temper.

"The seven Amazons of Tristaine's council are gathered." Shann drew the attention of the group as naturally as she drew breath. The traditional invocation fell pleasantly on Brenna's ears.

"We serve our clan as the living legacy of the Seven Sisters who gave it birth," Shann continued. "We call on their ancient wisdom, and the benevolent guidance of our Goddess, to preserve Tristaine through this long winter. But first, we invite them to join us for this lavish feast!"

The queen rubbed her hands together in gleeful greed, and Brenna's shoulders relaxed at the soft laughter that followed.

"Just let the uncouth among us," Aria said, eyeing Dana, "remember that only good little warriors get dessert." She swept to the altar in the center of the square and indicated the seven wooden bowls grouped on its surface. "In this case, a fiendishly creamy egg custard with fresh blackberries—"

Brenna was moving before any conscious thought registered, her eyes pinned on the altar. She brushed Aria roughly aside, snatched two of the bowls, and set them quickly on the rocky ground.

"Bren?"

She heard Jess, but for the second time that day, she ignored her. Brenna lowered another two bowls to the ground, then urgency stung her, and she swept the last three from the altar with her arm. Bowls bounced, and custard splattered over the rocky earth.

"Brenna." Jess was beside her, a hand on her shoulder.

"This is not a dessert tray." Brenna couldn't take her eyes from the ancient symbols carved in the altar's surface.

"Little sister?" Shann's touch was cool on her flushed face.

"This is a dark chancel," Brenna whispered. Her fingers trembled as they hovered over the glyphs. "We stand on blighted ground."

"Brenna!" Jess had heard enough. She took Brenna's shoulders in a firm grip and turned her from the altar, forcing her to meet her gaze. "Look at me, lass."

Brenna blinked. The fierceness in Jess's eyes broke through the fog clouding her mind, and she looked up at her in confusion. "What's a chancel?"

"Lady." Aria watched Brenna with dismay. "Please know I meant no disrespect to this place."

"Of course you didn't, adanin." Shann pressed Aria's hand, her eyes keen on Brenna's face. "Blades, are you all right?"

Brenna tore her gaze from Jess and crossed her arms as a shiver swept through her. She saw the six women circling the altar regarding her with a mix of worry and fascination. "Shann, I have no idea where that came from."

Shann's tone was low and calm. "Tell us what you remember, dear one."

"Did you hear that voice again?" Kyla's eyes were huge.

Dana stepped closer to her. "You look really strange, Brenna."

"No." Brenna shook her head. "No voice. Just a feeling when I saw those bowls...such outrage and fury..."

"I knew I should have made fruit pies," Aria whispered.

Brenna wiped her palms on her denim pants, and her mouth filled with saliva. "Hoo. This was a new one, folks. It wasn't...very pleasant. Excuse me."

She touched Jess's arm, then walked swiftly toward the trees lining the square. She was halfway there when the belly cramps struck, and she bent double and emptied her stomach violently.

Jess's arm was fast around her waist, and her callused hand brushed Brenna's hair back as she retched again. Brenna made the requisite indelicate spitting sounds until she could stand erect.

"Just breathe, adanin." Shann rubbed a small circular caress on her back.

"Yech," Brenna gasped. "Have I told you lately how—erk—much I hate throwing up, Jesstin?"

Jess looked too worried for a cavalier reply. "What ails her, lady?"

"Yet I keep doing it," Brenna finished, and spat again.

"It's to be expected, Jesstin." Shann wound her arm through Brenna's and walked her carefully back to the circle of Amazons around the altar. "Whatever strange force propelled Brenna to this altar had to be powerful indeed. Our young seer had no time to prepare herself, and her system took a bad shock. The body simply rebels at such invasion."

"But didn't she get invaded even worse earlier today?" Dana caught herself and looked around, but the faces turned to her were open and attentive. She swallowed. "That bully voice yelled at her to jump in the river, and she didn't get any advance warning then, either." Dana looked to Kyla for affirmation. "Right?"

"Yeah, Bren, and you weren't shook up like this

afterwards." Kyla folded her arms, a characteristic sign of her worry. "You were cold and drenched, but you didn't have this—haunted look."

Brenna's internal percolations had subsided enough that she could speak normally again. "That voice was nothing like this, Ky. This was pure rage, and there was nothing human in it. Or even animal. It was an energy I've never felt before. That's all I could catch, Shann."

"It's a beginning, Blades. Well done." Shann's finely veined hand moved over the rock surface of the altar. The Amazons fell silent as their queen's fingers brushed each glyph. "Many of these sigils are known to us," she murmured. "Others are alien to our clan."

She touched a familiar image, the crude two-headed ax that was an all but universal symbol of Amazon spirit. Near it were the simplistic circles within a circle of a bull's-eye target. Farther down the craggy stone were the intertwined ovals representing sexual love between women.

The altar held symbols for each of the seven guilds of Tristaine and more. The arrows in flight that Jess wore on her shoulder, marking her as a warrior. Other glyphs for healing, weaving, tilling the soil, spirituality. The intricate swirl of the artists' guild that Kyla wore on her flat stomach. The images weren't all identical to Tristaine's designs, but they were recognizable.

"What's this odd little corkscrew, lady?" Aria's perfectly manicured nail tapped one small carving in the stone. "Or this shooting flame thing?"

"We can only guess, adanin. I'll need our wisest historians to decipher them."

"Shift your bones, overgrown weed. She means me." Sarah tapped Jess's arm impatiently. "I'm the wisest historian Tristaine's got, madlady Artemis help us."

Jess moved respectfully aside to allow Sarah closer

access to the altar. She bent stiffly and peered at the symbols in baleful silence.

"All these are star glyphs," she said at last, her gnarled finger thumping the stone. "They stand for individual clans." Sarah squinted up at Dana. "Like our Seven Sisters, sprout. That star cluster up there that houses the souls of Tristaine's mothers."

Dana nodded, searching the dark sky for that well-loved array of twinkling lights. Kyla nudged her and pointed toward the opposite horizon, where she found them easily.

"Do you recognize any of these tribes, grandmother?" Shann asked.

"Not a one, lady." Sarah drew on her pipe and winced smoke out of one eye. "There's sigils here for magic, both light and dark. For queens and bloodletting."

Brenna's gaze fixed on those carvings, and she gave in to the persistent urge to step back from the altar. She noted the rest of the Queen's Council kept a prudent distance as well. To her pitched nerves, the black stone seemed to shimmer like a dark and malignant battery, vibrant with power.

Another hour of discussion brought them no closer to understanding their enemy, but at least it found them well fed. Weary of conjecture and sated with Aria's rich food, Shann's advisors sprawled in various stages of repose around a crackling fire.

Kyla drew a small cedar comb slowly through her curls, her eyes troubled and distant as she watched the flames. Shann and Sarah sat in private council, the smoke from Sarah's pipe wreathing their inclined heads.

Brenna lay with her head pillowed in Jess's lap, delicately licking the last spices off her fingers. "Ah, wee piggy," she burred, in a fair imitation of Jess's brogue, "ye did not die in vain."

Jess interrupted her constant scrutiny of the quiet square

to reach down and ruffle Brenna's hair. "You're a marvel, Bren. From spewing your guts to wolfing down half a roast boar in less time than it takes our fire to burn low."

It was true. Brenna's stomach was pleasantly full, with no lingering trace of its earlier rebellion. It seemed she had purged whatever toxin afflicted her, messily but efficiently.

"Well." Brenna fingered the collar of Jess's thick jacket. "I've heard Amazons are fast healers by necessity."

The gentle fingers in her hair lulled her, and Brenna's eyes drifted closed. Then she remembered this was only a break in the night's council, and she forced them open again. "Beautiful moon," she murmured.

Jess lifted her gaze to the night sky. "Aye, Selene's in her glory tonight."

"With the rising of the harvest moon, sisters, our Lady readies Herself for the celebration of Thesmophoria." Reclined on a warm fur near them, Aria followed their gaze. "Our festival menu will *not* include egg custard, in any form."

"Damn." Dana leaned closer to Kyla. "Is that Thesmie-whatsits some other Amazon big shot I'm supposed to know?"

"It's an old rite of our Nation, Dana." Jess's hand slipped beneath Brenna's hair and massaged the muscles of her neck. "We used to harvest our winter wheat at the rising of the Thesmophorian moon. It honors the goddess Demeter and her search for her kidnapped daughter, Persephone."

"She's the gal who ate the apple?" Dana's brow furrowed. "And got captured by the god of hell?"

"It was a pomegranate, Dana." Kyla snickered. "Persephone ate its seeds."

"And her imprisonment royally vexed her peace-loving mother." Aria smiled seductively at Dana, because that was how Aria smiled. "It's an immensely powerful time for Amazons, young one. A three-night festival of debauched revelry."

"A celebration might bring us together, Jess." Brenna lifted her head from the warrior's lap and sat up with a blissful stretch. "You think? A little dancing, a little wine..."

"Only a little wine, querida." Jess had gone back to scanning the square's perimeter with restless eyes. "Our warriors don't need much excuse these days to bash in each other's skulls."

Brenna nodded rueful agreement. She glanced at Aria's flagon of elderberry wine nearby, then looked away. She had not imbibed, in spite of a powerful temptation. Alcohol had played far too important a part in Brenna's life in the City, and she avoided it carefully now.

Gazing across the fire, she saw Dana staring down at the bench she shared with Kyla, her fingers curled around the small wooden comb Kyla had used earlier. Dana glanced surreptitiously at Kyla, then slipped the comb in her pocket and rested her hand over it. Brenna smiled.

She turned her head against the tree and studied the sculpted planes of Jess's profile, then caressed the powerful swell of her shoulder. In her mind's eye, Brenna could picture the glyph cresting that smooth muscle perfectly. She remembered the first time she had seen it, the night she met Jess.

The haggard Amazon prisoner, chained in a freezing cell in the City Clinic. Brenna's first medical intake in the Military Research unit. The brutal clinical trials Jess endured that left her bloody and battered, but unshakeable in her loyalty to Tristaine. Brenna's own hand, pressing the muzzle of a powerful stunner against the intricate tattoo on Jess's shoulder and firing an agonizing burst of electricity into the muscle.

Brenna shuddered and buried her face against the soft sheepskin of Jess's jacket.

"Hey. What's this?" Jess wrapped one arm around Brenna's shoulders. "You cold, lass?"

"Yeah," Brenna whispered and burrowed closer to the solid warmth that surrounded and shielded her through the bitterest of nights.

"Ah, young lust." Aria beamed at them with sentimental approval. "Jesstin, the sight of your macha self brings to mind, and to vulva, whole cadres of studly warriors who have heated my blankets—"

"Lady! *Shann!*"

Adrenaline sluiced through Brenna in a sick rush as they bolted to their feet. There was no mistaking the horror in that shouted alarm. She didn't recognize Vicar's voice until she staggered into the square, carrying a blood-soaked figure in her arms.

"Sweet Gaia, Vicar!" Shann ran to them, but Jess was faster. She lunged and caught the falling weight of the Amazon her cousin carried, and together they eased her onto the altar.

"Dana, bring torches!" Jess snapped. "Lady, it's Sirius."

Brenna actually needed this information. The gore covering the warrior rendered her all but unidentifiable. She moved quickly to stand at the altar across from Shann, to lend what assistance she could. She helped her unlace Sirius's vest and stared aghast at the bloody gashes and punctures that gaped like obscene eyes on her ebony torso.

Jess grasped Vicar's arm. "You hurt, Vic?"

She shook her head, then bent and rested her stained hands on her knees, her sides heaving for air. "Sirius guarded our south border tonight, Jesstin," she gasped. "I found her crawling toward the healers' lodge."

"Did she speak?"

"No, nothing, she just...stared at me."

"Lady, should I bring your satchel?" Kyla's voice was strained.

The queen's hands moved swiftly over her fallen warrior,

measuring her pulse at the neck, lifting an unresisting eyelid with great gentleness. Shann bent and smelled Sirius's faint breath, then straightened and met Brenna's stricken gaze.

Brenna had realized within seconds that even heroic efforts couldn't save this woman, and Shann had doubtless known it at first sight. A sick desolation filled her eyes. Kyla made a choked sound, and Dana's arm rose instinctively to encircle her shoulders.

"Assemble the guild, Vicar, battle ready." Jess's tone was low and firm. "I want a squad to guard our lady. And a full recon of the mesa, *now.*"

"Aye, Jesstin."

Brenna's heart gave a nasty lurch, and she whirled. "Jess? Sammy..."

"My adonai watches over the girl, Brenna, and she's well armed." Vic met Jess's sharp look and nodded. "We'll set a squad at the healing lodge as well." Vic spun and ran out of the square.

"Black-hearted, bile-swilling scrotes who did this..." Sarah's voice cracked.

Aria was pale as chalk. "There's nothing we can do, Shanendra?"

Shann didn't answer. The anguish faded from her eyes, and she looked down at the still face with quiet compassion. Raising one hand, she rested it at the base of Sirius's throat. Shann whispered an invocation, which Brenna recognized as the opening of one of the most sacred of Amazon traditions, the granting of the Queen's Blessing to a dying warrior.

Sirius had been mercifully unconscious until now, but at Shann's touch, her eyes opened slowly. Brenna tensed, but saw no indication of pain in Sirius's slack expression.

"Is she hurting, Bren?" Kyla whispered. She seemed oblivious to Dana's comforting arm.

"No, little sister." Brenna covered Kyla's hand with her

own. "She's leaving us, honey, and almost gone. She's not suffering."

"Jesstin." Dana swallowed visibly. "Should I join the recon—?"

"Quiet, adanin." Jess's tone was oddly gentle. "Stay. You should see this."

Shann looked into Sirius's eyes, and her lips lifted slightly in a smile. "Sirius, daughter of Shenoka, warrior of Tristaine," she said softly. "You close your eyes in the embrace of a clan that will cherish your memory. Tales of your courage will be told around our storyfires for generations. You gave your life protecting your sisters, and an Amazon can win no higher honor. You have the heartfelt gratitude of your queen, dear one."

Shann's slender fingers brushed the blood-soaked hair off Sirius's ashy brow, then carefully adjusted her head. Her dying eyes were clouding, but they focused briefly on a sight high above them.

Without looking, Brenna knew Shann had shifted Sirius's gaze so that the last view she had of the world would be the starfield of Tristaine's Seven Sisters. Brenna's vision trebled as her eyes brimmed with tears.

Sirius released one more shallow breath and was gone.

A soundless sigh passed through the women around the altar. Shann bowed her head and whispered a private prayer of farewell.

Brenna felt a warm stickiness on the side of her hand, and she blinked to clear her vision. The brutalized warrior had shed most of her blood in the forest, but the surface of the altar was still streaked with it. She saw, with a detached numbness, that several of the glyphs carved into the stone had filled with the sluggish red fluid.

J'heika, rise.

Brenna froze. Her gaze fastened on the simple target

glyph, the circles within a circle just visible beside the dead woman's knee.

The blood filling it was starting to boil.

"Shann," Brenna whispered.

Small red bubbles popped viciously in the roiling circles, and a thin, wisping tendril of steam curled from the center of the target. An acrid odor assaulted Brenna's nostrils, impossibly sharp given the fragile thread of vapor that carried it.

"This was a blood sacrifice," Brenna murmured.

Jess's voice reached her only faintly. "What do you mean, Bren?"

"Drawing first blood gives her ingress. It opens the portal between our worlds."

"Brenna!" Jess's tone was sharp now. "Look at me."

Brenna's mouth filled abruptly with a sour sulfur taste, and she stepped back in pure reaction.

Back and off the edge of the planet. Brenna slid bonelessly to the ground, Shann's cry reaching her dimly before all light vanished.

❖

She materialized seconds later in a nightmare of static.

Brenna opened her eyes on the pitched plane of another world glimpsed rarely, and only imperfectly, in her dreams. She was on her knees, grasping for purchase on a surface that wasn't grass or rock or anything else identifiable.

She sucked in a desperate breath, relieved but astonished to find oxygen was available on this harrowing plane. "Jesstin!" Brenna screamed. Her cry evaporated before reaching her own ears, lost in the erratic, pervasive buzzing filling the air.

All Brenna could see was a murky gray light, pulsing and surging all around her. This world seemed formless, with only vague black spikes far in the distance providing any solid contrast. But as her panic-filled eyes began to adjust and she forced herself to breathe slowly, Brenna saw a figure forming several feet in front of her.

It was a large human shape, its gender impossible to determine, as it was surrounded by a bristling nimbus of light that concealed its features. It took a step toward her, and Brenna skittered backward like a crab, on her hands and heels. She was picturing the hideous wounds inflicted on Sirius's body. But the looming figure stopped and lowered itself slowly to one knee before her. There was no menace or threat in its careful movements.

Brenna realized the ugly static buzzing in the air was fading a little. She made herself hold still as the glowing form extended an arm toward her. A rough hand materialized, still shrouded in light, but Brenna could see some details: long, strong fingers, a crude silver ring.

The hand clutched a small, leafy plant with gold berries that was instantly familiar. Brenna had last seen its kind in the abandoned cemetery beyond the mesa, adorning the graves of long-dead Amazon warriors. The connection was not a reassuring one.

Her eyes widened as a gold liquid welled from the spiked leaves of the plant, then overflowed it and spilled in a gentle stream to the ground. Abruptly, Brenna's throat seemed coated with dust, so deep was her thirst.

❖

Just as abruptly, her teeth clacked together as her butt hit the ground with jarring force.

Brenna's senses were assaulted at once with the chill night air of the village square and the alarmed shouts of the Amazons swarming around her. Regardless of her own perceptions, her sojourn to that strange spectral world had apparently lasted only long enough for her falling body to hit the sparse grass.

"Brenna!" Kyla's hands gripped her shoulders, and she blinked hard to focus on the frightened girl's face.

"I'm here, Ky," she gasped.

Instantly she felt a supporting warmth leave her back as Jess rose from behind Brenna and bolted toward the altar.

The night was shrill with the howling of the clan's dogs and the bugling of horses from the stables. The tumult disoriented Brenna, and it took her a moment to register the Amazons clustered at one end of the hulking black stone.

"Bren, you have to come." Kyla was obviously struggling for calm. She took Brenna's hands and hauled her bodily to her feet. "Hurry, adanin."

Brenna saw the woman splayed on the ground at the center of the group, and her heart trip-hammered in her breast as she raced toward her.

Shann lay motionless on her back, her eyes half-open, gazing sightlessly up at the Seven Sisters who rode high and unreachable over the heads of her embattled clan.

CHAPTER FIVE

Vitality surged at last through its withered limbs, and its tainted blood ignited with a stirring of ancient power. It had been sapping the energies of Tristaine's queen since she first entered the shadow cast by this mesa. Every spark of strength it drained from their pitiful ruler added to its own growing reserves.

Their queen had fallen so easily. This last tribe would prove little challenge to the divine destiny of an immortal sovereign. With the three-night reign of the Thesmophorian moon, the blood of these Amazons would soak this ground, and it would live again.

She who ruled the mesa centuries ago took form within the depths of the ebony altar. Not human form— that couldn't happen until the third Amazon tribe fell to its bloody will.

But the essence of Woman filled it again and restored its betrayed gender. The Feminine force, pure and strong and good in Tristaine's queen, became a potent malevolence in an immortal sorceress held captive by death for hundreds of years.

She had leeched enough of the queen's vitality for now. She wanted the old woman alive at the rising of the harvest moon. Her bloody death would be delectable, a death to savor through the thousand years of her reign.

Her imprisonment had ended. She was Botesh, and she would rule again.

❖

No evident blood loss. Pulse thready. Febrile. Respiration shallow but even.

With burning eyes, Brenna scanned her initial entry, made hours ago, after her first thorough examination of the unconscious queen. Her gaze drifted over the rough-hewn log wall of the healing lodge to its window, and she saw no hint yet of approaching dawn. Scrubbing her tousled hair off her forehead, she bent over her journal again.

Shann's still unresponsive. And I can find no medical reason in the world for this unbroken sleep.

Jess has posted sentries around the perimeter of the village. Our warriors saw no sign of intrusion, no tracks left by enemies. Sirius wasn't mauled by any animal we've seen in these hills, but we still don't know what killed her. Brenna closed her eyes for a moment. *I'm terrified.*

She closed her journal and rose from the wooden stool, feeling the endless day in her aching knees and stiff neck. She glanced down at the pallet where Shann lay, her elegant hands still on the warm blankets covering her. Her lips were parted with her quick breath, and dark circles bracketed her closed eyes.

Brenna drew aside the clicking strings of beads that curtained the window. The torches posted outside the lodge cast a reddish light on the many Amazons standing vigil around it, awaiting news of their queen.

She felt the comfort of Jess's presence behind her first, then the relief of her strong hands targeting perfectly the tight muscles in her neck. Brenna let her head drop forward, allowing those talented thumbs to probe deeply, releasing her tension in warm waves.

"You have to rest, Bren."

"Soon," Brenna murmured, soaking in the familiar texture of those callused hands on her skin.

"You've done all anyone can for our lady." Jess's strong fingers explored the curves of her shoulders and upper back. "You'll do Shann no good by wearing yourself out, lass."

Brenna leaned back against her, folding Jess's arms over her breasts. "I wish she could tell me what to do, Jesstin."

"You're a fine healer, adonai. Shann knows that." Jess rested her chin on top of Brenna's head, both of them gazing out the beaded window into the night. "But more than illness afflicts our lady. We'll need your gifts as a seer as much as your skills in healing to save her."

"No pressure, of course." Brenna meant to speak lightly, but she felt weak tears filling her eyes again. For the third time that day. Incredible. She should start keeping track in her journal of the number of times she either cried or threw up in service to her clan. She wanted the final tallies inscribed on her gravestone.

"Brenna." The voice was muted and slightly hoarse.

Jess released her, and Brenna moved quietly across the large room to the pallet where Samantha lay. She sat on its edge and looked carefully at her sister's pale face. "Hey, Sammy. It's awful late. Why are you awake?"

Samantha's eyes were on the still figure on the other bed, and a line appeared between her brows. "Is she dying? Your friend."

"No." Brenna shivered. "I don't really know. I'm not sure what's wrong with her."

"You'll figure it out." Sammy turned her remote gaze on Brenna. "You were the best medic in the Clinic. Maybe in the whole City."

This simple declaration of faith almost brought on the tears again. Brenna laid her fingers on Sammy's throat to measure her pulse. The candlelight illuminated a thin scar that etched the delicate skin of her neck, and Brenna caught her breath. "What did this, Sam?"

"I was kept on a leash in Prison." She delivered this information with the same dispassionate voice that asked about Shann. Brenna stared at her in shock, and Sammy turned her face from her sister's touch—not angrily or abruptly, but a subtle distancing. "And that's Jesstin? The one who pulled us out of the river?"

Jess stepped out of the shadows, her hands crossed on her belt. "Aye, Samantha, I'm Jess."

Brenna wrapped a cup of cool water in Samantha's hand to ease her throat, and she sipped it as she regarded Jess. "They still talk about you in the City. How you and Brenna broke out of the Clinic together."

Jess nodded.

"You two are married now, Brenna said."

"Your blood sister and I are adonai, lass." Jess's tone was kind, but she studied Sammy as carefully as Sammy watched her. "It's our word for lifemate."

"Adonai." Samantha nodded and gazed at Brenna silently for a moment. "Do the Amazons have a word for widow?"

Brenna swallowed and met Jess's gaze.

"Dolore," Jess said quietly.

Samantha's lips moved silently as she repeated the word, and her eyes closed.

"You should get some sleep." Brenna took the cup and rose from the side of the pallet, her movements gentle, not wanting to startle her. "I'll be right over there if you need anything."

"Bree?" Sammy's cold fingers on Brenna's wrist stopped her. "Your friend was kind to me earlier. I hope she'll be okay."

"Me too." Brenna hesitated, then bent and rested her

lips briefly on her sister's forehead, a lifetime of loving her overriding any fear of rejection. Brenna patted Jess's arm absently on her way back to Shann, then began checking her vital signs again. Respiration, pulse, still slightly feverish...

Jess waited patiently until Brenna opened her journal to re-record the same readings. Then she unlatched the door of the lodge and walked out onto the wooden porch. The Amazons standing outside in the predawn chill stirred and turned toward Jess, and she lifted a hand in reassurance. "Our queen rests comfortably, adanin. There's no change." Jess's voice was rough with fatigue. Her eyes searched the crowd. "Aria?"

Aria emerged into the torchlight in a whirl of colorful silk. "Jesstin?"

"Join us, please." Jess motioned Aria into the lodge before her, then secured the door again. She took Aria's elbow and escorted her to Shann's pallet, and Brenna blinked up at them, puzzled.

"You've passed a harrowing night as well, Aria." Jess studied her friend's face. "Do you have the energy for a few hours' watch?"

Aria's sculpted eyebrows arched, and she rested a hand on a curvaceous hip. "I'm sure my rickety old crone bones can withstand such strenuous labor, lamb chop, yes."

"Good." Jess held her hand out to Brenna. "This one's sleeping now."

"Jess," Brenna protested. "I just want to see if—"

"Aria will guard our lady's sleep, Brenna, and your sister's." Jess lifted Brenna to her feet. "I'll watch over yours."

"But—"

"Call us if they stir, adanin." Jess drew Brenna to the empty pallet Shann often slept on when an injured Amazon needed her care.

Brenna had more objections half-formed in her mind as

Jess eased her down onto the cool bed, but the words faded before they passed her lips. Jess climbed carefully on the pallet behind her and wrapped her long arms around Brenna's waist. Spooning was all they had room for, and everything they needed most.

Brenna yawned hugely. "Ah int ucker ace is ime."

Jess smiled into her hair. "Once again?"

"Aria didn't suck your face this time." Brenna nestled back into the warmth of the powerful body enfolding hers. "Did you two have a fight?"

"She ravished me on the porch." Jess's breath tickled her ear. "I'll be bearin' her bairn come spring."

Brenna snickered, but then remembered their most urgent need. "Jess. We need to find the plant that glowing giant showed me—"

"We'll not find it without sunlight, querida." Jess kissed the top of Brenna's head. "Tomorrow will be trial enough, but it's hours away. Rest with me a while."

Brenna felt her body relax into a boneless mass, and her eyes drifted closed.

Their queen on the brink of coma. Tristaine under siege by some demon force. Her adored little sister destroyed by grief. And in these arms, against all sane expectation, Brenna found safety and peace.

"Jesstin."

"Hm."

"I cherish you," Brenna whispered.

Jess went still behind her. Then she cradled the side of Brenna's face The light of Selene's ghostly moon began to fade as they drifted to sleep beneath the protective watch of their sisters.

❖

Bracken at a quick trot was smoother and easier on Brenna's spine than most horses at a leisurely lope. She knew Jess had taken some ribbing three years ago when she picked the scruffy little foal out of Tristaine's herd as her personal mount. Only Hakan, the clan's stablemaster, had grinned at Jess in approval. She knew mountain mustangs had unquenchable heart and, more often than not, could run brawnier stallions into the ground.

Jess slowed Bracken to a walk as they wound through the thinning trees at the base of the mesa, and Brenna tried to curb her impatience. She tightened her arms around Jess's waist and scanned the ground carefully, searching for the gold berries and silver leaves of the plant from her vision.

Shann had been no better or worse after the sun rose that morning. But the longer her strange sleep lasted, the greater the chance she would never wake. Brenna held fast to the hope that the odd shrub she'd been shown could save their queen.

"You know, butch of mine," Brenna knocked politely on Jess's back, "we could cover a lot more territory if you'd let me ride my own horse. Hakan could pick me out a nice, gentle—"

"Chipmunk," Jess finished. "You'll ride nothing larger until the clan's safe again, Bren."

Brenna squeaked in outrage. "Hey, you saw me ride yesterday! Bracken and I booked, and I stuck to his back like a—"

"Aye, I saw you ride, and that's why you'll be astride chipmunks." Jess checked the position of the sun and turned slightly east. "Until I know you won't bolt off on a wild hair again, with a great flailin' of elbows and buttocks—"

"Yahhh." Brenna curved her hands into claws and dragged them down Jess's chest in mock fury. "You better be nicer to me if you want any buttocks at all in your immediate future. And Jess..." She leaned out slightly, to see her lover's face. "You don't get to decide when I'm ready for a new challenge. I'm the only one who can know that. Right?"

Jess's expression softened. "Aye, Bren. You're right. I thank you for letting me butch you on this, just for now."

Brenna nodded, content, and went back to scanning the greenery around them. Still no sign of their mystery plant.

"As for covering ground, we have our two sisters to broaden our search." Jess shaded her eyes to see the distant figures of Kyla and Dana, their horses moving in tandem toward the deeper forest. "Ears."

Grateful for the warning, Brenna quickly covered her ears before Jess unleashed a piercing whistle through two fingers. The far-off figures stopped, and Dana lifted one arm to indicate their direction. Kyla reached out and adjusted her arm slightly, and Jess grinned and signaled agreement.

"They seem to be spending a lot of time together, those two," Brenna observed as Jess nudged Bracken into a lope to join their friends.

"Mostly Dana's doing, I think. Seeing Sirius die was hard on Ky. Her heart's not ready to risk much right now."

"And she'll choose her time to face new challenges." Brenna rested her cheek against Jess's warm back. "Some macha butch taught me that."

The terrain they covered couldn't have changed much since the previous day, but as they neared the secluded graveyard, Brenna found the forest around them increasingly ominous. The sun-dappled trees seemed to watch their passage, as if to ensure these intruders entered hallowed ground with a proper respect.

In the distance, Brenna glimpsed the low rock wall that encircled the cemetery and was surprised by a faint superstitious dread. She was a healer. She had intimate knowledge of the messy workings of the human body and had never held illusions about death. But since she had found Tristaine, a series of quite vivid visions had been forced on Brenna, and the last of her City-trained skepticism was crumbling. She would never see death and the realms that lay beyond it in simplistic terms again.

When they reached the wall, Jess extended her left arm, and Brenna grasped it and slid to the ground. Jess lifted one long leg over her horse's neck and landed lightly beside her. She took Brenna's hand as they stepped over the stone enclosure, and neither felt inclined to let go.

Brenna let out a long breath, seeing the gold-berried plant everywhere now, dotting grave after grave in the barren yard. "These things had to be transplanted here, Jess. They can't be native to these hills, or we'd see them everywhere."

"The Amazons who settled the mesa may have cultivated this strain in their gardens." Jess knelt and fingered the silver-veined leaves of one small sprig. "For this one purpose, to guard the sleep of their warriors. They seem to flourish without tending." She stood and brushed the sandy soil from her hands.

They walked slowly among the canted gravestones. "The worms crawl in, the worms crawl out," Brenna murmured.

"Sorry?" Jess bent closer.

"Oh, one of the charming chants that went around the County Home where Sam and I grew up." Brenna rubbed Jess's muscled forearm with her free hand. "No one really knew what it meant. Bodies aren't allowed to decay in the City. There aren't any cemeteries there anymore."

"No? How do they honor their dead in the City?"

"They dispose of them efficiently. Same way they handle their living."

Jess waited.

"She blames me, Jess."

"Ah, lass." She wound an arm around Brenna's shoulders. "Your Sammy's too full of pain to see things clearly right now."

"I'm not so sure about that." Brenna folded her arms, hugging herself. "She was making it, Jesstin. Even in that sterile hell down there, Sammy carved out some happiness. She had a loving husband, a job. She was starting a family. I wrecked all that. Caster never would have targeted her if she hadn't hated me so—"

"Brenna." Jess stopped her and took her shoulders gently. "*Caster* destroyed your sister's happiness. Just as her kind has brutalized and laid waste to thousands of innocent lives for generations in the City. Caster deserves all your rage, adonai, and all the blame. Sammy will know that someday."

Brenna studied Jess's face, wanting to believe her. Jess tipped her chin with one finger, then lowered her head to kiss her with a light, searching warmth. The city of the dead around them faded for a moment. As the love between them deepened, their physical intimacy had developed its own diverse language. This feathered brushing of lips offered comfort and solace, and Brenna drank it gratefully.

Then she almost bit Jess's tongue as a piercing whistle split the air.

Jess whipped around and targeted its source, then grasped Brenna's hand and took off on a run. Sorry, sorry, sorry, Brenna apologized silently, every time they leaped over a headstone, her heart hammering in her chest. They reached the far end of the stone wall and jumped it, then crashed through a haze of tangled brush.

"Dana!" Jess barked.

"We're here, Jesstin."

Brenna heard no great alarm in Dana's voice, and a moment later Jess batted some hanging branches aside and they saw her. She looked whole enough, as did Kyla, and Brenna's relief was immediately tinged with annoyance. Just like the time Sammy had scared her when they were kids by running too close to a busy street, she wanted to hug her sisters, then slap them silly for frightening her like that.

Jess apparently felt some of the same mixed maternal urge. She set her hands on her hips and glared at Dana, panting. "A fine, clear signal, adanin, but that particular whistle warns of *attack*. If there's no danger—"

"I figured you'd want to see this pretty quick." Dana hadn't turned to look at them, and neither had Kyla. Brenna followed their gaze and went still.

Several yards away, the brush had been scraped clean in a rough oval. In the center of the hard-packed earth stood a sculpture, cut in one piece from a large block of black granite. It was a life-sized depiction of two women—one kneeling, the other draped full-length across her lap.

"Sweet Lady," Jess whispered, and Brenna reached for her hand again.

Whoever sculpted this piece had been no master. There was little detail hewn into the rock, and its planes were rough and unfinished. But somehow that starkness made the impact of the image all the more powerful.

There was enough nuance to see that the kneeling figure was a very old woman, her face lined with both age and sorrow. The folds of her robes draped over the naked body cradled in her lap, a younger woman of obvious strength, and obviously lifeless. Her hand lay loose around the hilt of a crude sword.

It was a classic image, emblematic of the pietas created by any number of civilizations. The archetype of the female mourning her fallen.

The almost featureless face of the old woman somehow conveyed the depths of her grief as she gazed down at the slain warrior. Her gnarled hand rested at the base of the dead woman's throat. The one clear detail on the back of the elder's hand was the simple glyph that also graced Shann's shoulder— the mark of an Amazon queen.

An image rose in Brenna's mind—the sketch she'd made

in her journal of Shann cradling a dying child.

Jess lowered herself to one knee as she stared at the roughcast figures, and her eyes glittered with tears.

Dana looked from her commander to Brenna uneasily, as if she wanted to offer comfort.

Kyla walked quietly to Jess, knelt beside her, and rested her head against her shoulder.

Brenna's throat ached, and she had to look away from this primitive but eloquent rendering of the Queen's Blessing. Only then did she register what should have been immediately evident—the ground around the sculpture was thickly carpeted with the gold-berried plants.

"Why did they put this...shrine outside of the cemetery?" Dana's tone was subdued. "We never would have seen it if we hadn't come up this way."

Brenna cupped her elbows in her hands, her eyes drawn irresistibly to the stone figure of the warrior. Such a powerful body, slack and empty in death. Its proportions were so similar to Jess's tall frame that a chill chased up her back.

"We'd best get what we came for, Bren." Jess's head rested in Kyla's auburn curls.

Brenna stepped forward carefully, laying a hand on Jess's shoulder as she passed. She kept her gaze on the largest of the plants, growing lush at the center of the base of the granite sculpture. Its gold berries were glossy in the midst of the silver-veined leaves.

Not looking at the stone faces in front of her, Brenna knelt to grasp the stem. It was wiry and full in her fingers, and its roots went deep. She pulled gently, smoothly, and at last felt the thready tearing of the soil surrendering its hold.

"J'heika..."

Brenna started, and her eyes flew to the ancient rock face of the Amazon queen. She rose on unsteady legs, the plant clenched in one hand. "No," she whispered.

The title had been spoken softly, with great tenderness. And with heartrending regret. The voice was unmistakable.

"J'heika, rise," Shann whispered from the ancient stone lips. *"Forgive me, Brenna."*

Brenna felt the blood drain from her face. She breathed deeply until the dizziness passed and she could turn and face her sisters.

"We need to go home," she said quietly.

CHAPTER SIX

B renna saw Vicar's tall roan loping toward them as they turned onto the path leading up to the mesa. Vic raised a hand and called something she couldn't hear, but relief was already flooding through Brenna. Vic was grinning like a bandit.

"Our lady's awake, Jesstin!" Vicar spun her horse neatly as she reached them, skittering gravel and dust. "Weak as a pup, but all her senses intact. She's asking for our seer, here."

"Good news, cousin." Jess tapped a knee to Bracken's side, and he lunged up the rocky trail, followed closely by the rest of their party.

They cantered minutes later into the village square, which was milling with women talking in excited groups. Several ran to greet them, and Brenna saw her relief mirrored in their upturned faces.

The news of Shann's collapse had shaken the clan badly. Tristaine had never been an idle tribe, and this sunny day should have found the Amazons busy with the work of their seven guilds. The warriors were on duty guarding the mesa, but no cloth was being spun, no food preserved, or horses trained. The routine of daily life had come to a halt until the fate of their queen was known.

When they reached the healing lodge, Jess slithered from Bracken's back and lifted Brenna down. Several women were clustered around the door to the cabin, but they cleared a respectful path, hands reaching out to touch them.

"She's back with us, Jesstin!"

"Aye, Keyen."

"Our lives for her, Jess."

"Always." Jess opened the door and ushered Brenna, Kyla, and Dana into the lodge. "Give us a moment with our lady, adanin."

Brenna waited for her eyes to adjust to the lamplit dimness of the cabin. Kyla had no such patience. She was on her way to the raised pallet where Shann lay before Jess had the door latched.

Kyla sat carefully on the edge of the bed and rested her head on Shann's breast with a tired sigh. The queen opened her eyes and focused on the women watching her, and the corner of her mouth lifted. She patted Kyla's shoulder with maternal affection.

Aria rose from her chair in the corner and shocked Dana to speechlessness with a smacking kiss of greeting. "I believe you'll find Shanendra much improved, my sweet sistren. Brenna, dearest, I'll go check on young Samantha, who lunches with Vicar's adonai. Lovely woman, Wai Li, though her gravies just miss proper texture."

"Our thanks, Aria." Jess gave Aria's buttock a friendly pat before she swept out of the cabin, then she grinned at Brenna. Shann's revival had lifted the burden on her broad shoulders enough to allow such teasing.

"I'm sorry I worried you, little Ky." Shann's voice was raspy, and Dana all but trotted to pour her water from the jug by her pallet.

"Worried me," Kyla murmured. "You about stopped my damn heart, lady. I swear I'm going to have you impeached or impounded or dethroned or something, if you ever do this to us again."

"Tell me how you feel, Shann." Brenna shrugged off the canvas satchel she carried and sat at her other side. She took

Shann's wrist to measure her pulse. Shann's color was better than this morning, and she seemed fully alert. Brenna was still faintly nauseous with relief. She wondered if throwing up on Tristaine's queen could be counted on her final sacrifice-for-the-clan tally.

"I feel like that accursed altar dropped on my head." Shann frowned. "Just how much of Aria's elderberry wine did I swill at last night's council?"

Jess studied her with folded arms. "What do you remember, lady?"

"I remember blessing Sirius." Shann accepted the mug of water from Dana and drank deeply. "I remember seeing Brenna's eyes roll back in her head. Then nothing."

"Do you have pain anywhere?" Brenna moved a lantern closer to illuminate her features.

"Nothing worth mentioning, Blades, just a bit stiff." Shann lifted a hand to forestall the next question. "Can we move past my humiliating royal infirmity for the moment, please, and address the welfare of our clan? Jesstin, your report."

"There've been no other incidents, Shann. We scouted the mesa thoroughly and found nothing. I've doubled the watch at all sectors, and our guild remains on full alert."

Shann nodded. "Kyla, your take on our adanin?"

Kyla sat up slowly, and Brenna could see the lines of strain around her eyes. "We're all mourning Sirius, lady. Rumors are everywhere. Some worry Caster survived the flood, and she's after us again. Or there's some random tribe of cutthroats out to get us. Others think Tristaine is still under that stupid bloody curse I've never believed in. Our enemy is invisible, and our sisters are scared."

"Rational enough." Shann gently tapped Brenna's hand off her forehead. "I'm not feverish, adanin. Sweet Artemis, Jesstin, what must she be like when you're ill?"

"She hovers like a buzzard, lady."

Brenna glared at Jess, who winked at her.

"Dana?" With an effort, Shann sat up straighter against the folded furs cushioning her back. "Your thoughts on our council, please."

Dana had retreated respectfully to one corner, and now her eyebrows shot up. She looked at Jess and stepped closer to Shann's bed. "Well, I don't know anything about Amazon curses. But it seems to me this place is haunted. I mean, we've got blood-steam rising out of that spooky-as-shit altar out there. And Brenna getting possessed by all these voices. I don't think we should waste any time hunting down a human enemy. Whatever conked you guys out last night sure wasn't that. Human." Dana swallowed and glanced at Jess again.

"A fair analysis, adanin. Thank you." Shann smiled at Dana and cleared her throat. "All right. Our first priority is to bring our women together. I want a full clan assembly early this evening. Our sisters have the right to know what little we've learned so far."

"Shann. Are you sure you're up to a big gathering?" Brenna was prepared to brave any further reference to hovering buzzards. "Come on. You were all but comatose for a good twelve hours."

"I know, Bren." Shann sighed. "And I still feel bloody wiped, I admit it. But, yes, I do have the strength for this because it needs doing. Now, adanin, we have hours before dusk, which I will spend obediently resting. Jesstin will want to run a circuit of the mesa and check in with her warriors."

"Aye, Shann."

"Dana, spread the word of tonight's meeting, please. And Kyla, love, please disperse that mob of hovering buzzards from the front porch. Tell our sisters their queen expects to see them busy and productive until sunset, or heads will most surely fly."

"They'll quail in terror, Shann." Kyla smiled at her lovingly and kissed her cheek. "But they'll step right smart, too. Your word compels us."

"Yes, in this and all things." Shann eased back against the furs and pressed Brenna's hand. "Will you stay a moment, Blades? For private council."

"I'd be honored." Brenna felt Jess's finger brush her face, and she smiled up at her. "See you soon, hotshot."

"Lady." Jess nodded at Shann and herded Dana and Kyla out of the healing lodge.

Brenna sighed, content to regard the queen in silence as long as she allowed it. The grieving message that had drifted from the stone sculpture in Shann's voice still haunted her. Brenna told herself, with every league that passed beneath Bracken's hooves on their way back to the mesa, that it hadn't been a farewell. Now she drank in Shann's face—the laugh lines etched around her kind eyes, the slight smile on her lips—with simple pleasure.

"It's my turn to hover, little sister." Shann's gaze turned appraising. "My slumber was deep and dreamless, but I wasn't the only one knocked senseless by that scary-as-shit altar out there." Shann managed a fair imitation of Dana's voice, but then her smile faded. "What happened to you, Brenna?"

"I guess I have to call it a vision." Brenna closed her eyes, remembering. "Some strange, chaotic world, hardly more than a gray blur. There was an ugly buzzing sound, but I couldn't see what caused it."

She gave as clear an account as possible of her time in that odd world and the light-drenched giant she encountered there. She was careful to keep her report linear and factual, but when she was finished, Shann studied her thoughtfully.

"And what was your heart telling you, Blades? That information may be just as vital as the testimony of your eyes."

"Well." Brenna swallowed. "I was scared out of my head. First of how strange everything was, that awful static, and I couldn't see anything. Then of the giant. But when she—or he—reached toward me, I stopped being scared. And not because she was holding that plant instead of a weapon. I just knew she wouldn't hurt me. There was some kind of... benevolence, there."

"Good." Shann traced Brenna's wrist with her thumb, apparently lost in thought.

"Hey—the plant, we found it." Brenna started out of her memories and reached for the canvas bag she'd dropped at the foot of Shann's pallet. She lifted it into her lap and carefully withdrew the lush plant, its roots wrapped in soft parchment soaked in water from her canteen. "I was hoping that giant spirit showed it to me because it might help you, that it was medicinal. We've only seen it growing in that cemetery."

"You see this shrub everyday, Brenna, here in Tristaine." Shann fingered the gold berries with something like reverence. "Every time you pass my lodge, where all the glyphs of our clan are etched above my door. But you see only a stylized rendering. This plant is part of the design of the glyph worn by our clan's seers."

Brenna blinked. "Our seers?"

"You being our only one, at the moment." Shann turned the cutting carefully in her hands to examine its leaves. "Tristaine passed long generations without birthing anyone gifted with your second sight. I've never laid eyes on this plant in nature, Brenna. Finding it is a true blessing."

"Then it's not used for healing?"

"It's a narcotic. And an hallucinogen. Our seers used it much as other cultures used peyote or certain mushrooms. It induces trance and opens doors to other planes."

"Oh." Brenna's voice squeaked a bit. "Then it's for me?"

Shann pursed her lips. "Tell me again how you felt in your vision when you first touched this plant?"

Brenna sighed. "Thirsty."

"It's for you."

Brenna stared at the spiked leaves in Shann's fingers. "Okay," she said finally. "I'll do it. Another trance, a little nap. I can handle that."

"We need to move quickly, Blades. Tonight, after the assembly."

"Okay."

"Set this in water for now." Shann rested her head back against the furs as Brenna arranged the plant in a pitcher and placed it on a table that caught sunlight from the beaded window. "A giant spirit," she murmured.

"I'm sorry?" Brenna sat on the pallet again.

"You described her well, Bren. That she was."

"Who?" Brenna was puzzled. "Are you talking about the giant I saw in the vision?"

"You saw her there." Shann lifted Brenna's hand again and smoothed her fingers on the soft blanket. "You heard her when your blood sister cast herself into the river. And she came to you seasons ago, just before the flood covered Tristaine."

Troubled, Brenna focused on Shann's hands and the simple silver ring she wore on her middle finger. She'd seen its twin before on a large, spectral hand outlined in light.

"Dyan," she whispered.

"Dyan." The name was a prayer on Shann's lips.

They sat quietly for a while. Around them, Tristaine was coming to life again. Horses trumpeted from the stables, hammers mended railings, voices called to each other.

"Lady?"

"Yes, Bren."

"We found a sculpture outside the cemetery. It depicted the Queen's Blessing. And the Amazon queen...she spoke to me. In your voice."

"Mine?" Shann's brows rose. "What did she say?"

"J'heika, rise." Brenna paused. "And you asked me to forgive you."

Shann's gaze drifted toward the window. "I can't fathom this message, adanin. But I'll rest on it. It's one more piece of a puzzle we must solve quickly if we're to preserve our clan."

Brenna nodded, then got up and smoothed the blankets over Shann's shoulders. "I'll call someone to bring you a light supper, Shann, and sit with you while you rest. I don't want to hear of you twitching before sundown."

"Yes, ma'am." Shann smiled. "No twitching."

Brenna checked the plant in its patch of sunlight, then went to the door. Glancing back, she saw a tear forming a silver trail down Shann's cheek.

"Lady?" she called softly. "Are you in pain?"

Shann shook her head, eyes closed. "No, loved one. It's probably a...a perimenopausal hormone surge. It's just...ah, Bren."

Brenna waited.

"I so wish she could have come to me," Shann whispered. Her head settled deeper into the furs as she drifted into sleep.

Brenna lowered her eyes and stepped quietly out of the lodge. She blinked at the clouded sunlight of midday, her mind churning with lost love and evil altars and the trial that awaited her when the moon rose.

A prospect made all the more daunting by the sick certainty in Brenna's gut. She knew, as surely as she knew she loved Jess, that Shann had understood the stone queen's message. And she'd lied about it.

❖

She didn't like being separated from Jess.

Brenna had never been the clingy type. And accusations

of hovering aside, she was usually able to suppress her more florid imaginings of disaster, even where her lifemate was concerned. But as Brenna moved through the village, she still searched constantly for Jess, who was riding a check of the mesa and wouldn't be back any time soon. That knowledge didn't ease Brenna's craving to see her. An image of Sirius's brutalized body flashed through her mind, and she shuddered.

She was stopped frequently by Amazons wanting to hear the latest on Shann or ask questions about that night's clan council. When did this happen, Brenna wondered. When did I become a trusted source to these fierce, amazing women?

She remembered her first days in Tristaine. Reeling with culture shock and the trauma of the Clinic, Brenna had doubted she would ever find acceptance in Jess's clan. Shann's faith in her had helped, as had the friendship of Kyla and Camryn, and the strong, steady beat of Jess's heart beneath her cheek as they slept peaceful nights beneath Tristaine's Seven Sisters.

Brenna stopped short as a gaggle of children passed in front of her, herded with loving sternness by women from the guild of mothers. She grinned at one toddler who seemed fixated on inserting her finger into as many ears as possible, and returned the waves of the older kids. The clan's young all idolized Jess, and Brenna enjoyed basking in the warmth of her reflected glory.

She folded her arms, watching the small crew scramble its way to the dining hall, and a kind of wistfulness filled her. She thought of Vicar's infant son and the sweetness of his downy head cradled in the palm of her hand. Brenna and her sisters would watch this boy grow into puberty, then tell him good-bye. These partings were often wrenching for all involved, but they were a necessary part of Amazon culture.

Brenna had never considered bearing a child. Childbirth was regulated by the City as strictly as all other human endeavors. Genetic screenings had to be passed and permits secured. Brenna had assumed that her single-minded focus on her career would eclipse any hope for family life. And in her heart, she would have feared for any child in her care. During her last year in the City, she had spent too much time in an alcohol-induced haze to be trusted with an infant.

Brenna's gaze drifted from the children to a young mother whose arms would always ache with the memory of a lost baby. Samantha sat cross-legged on the low stone wall that separated the village square from the cabins beyond it, seeming oblivious to the activity around her, or the chill breeze that swept the square. She was curled around something she held in her hand, and Brenna saw a small flash of flame from a match.

"Since when do you *smoke*?"

So ingrained was her reaction to her older sister's voice, Sammy actually whipped the hand-rolled cigarette out of her mouth and hid it behind her back. Jess would have found the resemblance between them striking as she glared back at Brenna.

"Since when do you creep up on a person like a damn *ghost*?" Sammy snapped. She drew the cigarette out again and looked at it dismally. It was a flaking mess.

Brenna uncrossed her arms and sat on the wall beside her sister, leaving a careful distance between them. "Sheesh, you used to be so healthy, Sam. You always nagged *me* about nutrition and exercise."

"Yeah, well, someone had to nag you." Samantha scowled, trying to roll the shredded tobacco and paper back into some semblance of a tube. "You take terrible care of yourself."

Not necessarily true anymore, Brenna thought. "Where did you get that, anyway?"

"An older bald lady who smokes a pipe." Sammy squinted at her work. "I asked her for it. She called me a weed."

Brenna muttered imprecations against Sarah in her head, but managed to smother further criticism as her sister succeeded in lighting up. She took the time to study her. Samantha's eyes had lost some of that frightening blankness, but her face was pale and drawn even in the chill breeze of afternoon. "How do you feel, Sammy?"

"I'm all right." Samantha scraped tobacco off the tip of her tongue with one fingernail. "I'm sorry I made you guys jump into that river after me. You don't swim very well."

"You don't swim at all." Brenna risked touching her hand. "You were trying to kill yourself, Sam."

"Not really." Sammy blew out a plume of smoke and coughed, her eyes distant. "Or not on purpose. I just wanted to rest. I've been so tired."

"Tired?" Brenna moved closer to her, anxiety sharpening her voice. "You wanted to die because you were *tired*?"

"Don't be stupid, Brenna." Samantha's tone was suddenly entirely adult. "I don't have to explain myself to you anymore. Karen and Lee Ann were gone, my baby and Matt were gone, and finding you just didn't seem so—"

"Wait a minute. Slow down." Brenna gripped her shoulder. "Who's Karen? Who's Lee Ann?"

Sammy blinked, then stared at the glowing cigarette in her fingers. "Karen was my legal defender in the City. Lee Ann was her partner. They were both Amazon-crazy. They ate up all the rumors about Tristaine." Grief filled Samantha's eyes. "They got me out of the Prison. And gave up everything they had to do it, too. The City would have killed them if they were caught. They came with me to find you and the Amazons."

"What happened to them, Sammy?"

Samantha didn't answer at once. The silence spun out between them, and in spite of the tension in her gut, Brenna let it linger. She was beginning to see the first hints of the expressive sister she knew in the myriad of emotions passing over Sammy's face.

"They were like a couple of kids." The corner of Samantha's mouth lifted. "Both of them were older than me, but I felt like their mother sometimes. They were so excited about Tristaine. And they were so sappy in love. That was hard. I missed Matt so much."

Samantha's eyes filled, and Brenna took her hand.

"It was pretty hard travel. Karen and Lee Ann knew more about the mountains than I did, but we all grew up in the City. We weren't real prepared. We kept running out of food. Karen got these awful blisters." Samantha shivered and tucked her free hand beneath her arm to warm it. "But we found the maps the Amazons left in each of their camps. They kept us going. Half the time we could see a trail to follow from all of you passing through. It was such a...different world for me, all that sky. Sometimes I'd go whole hours without remembering."

Brenna murmured something. No real words, just a soft sound of encouragement.

"Lee Ann fell from a high ridge about two-thirds of the way up the south face. Karen died trying to save her."

"Ah, Sam." Brenna let out a long breath. She had seen that ridge awash in Amazon blood in one of her dreams, when the women of Tristaine had climbed the mountain pass last summer. Shann had heeded her warning to avoid it. Taking that route had shortened Samantha's journey to the mesa, but at a hideous cost. "I'm so sorry about your friends. They were Amazons from the day they were born, and we'll add their names to Tristaine's roster of our honored fallen."

Samantha stared at her. "You're different here, Bree, aren't you?"

Brenna thought about it. "Yeah. I am different. I've changed a lot since we last saw each other."

"You look stronger."

"I am."

"Physically and otherwise."

"And otherwise." Brenna nodded.

"No booze?"

"No." She dropped her eyes, regretting the dozen times her younger sister had seen her drunk. She'd never been raucous or belligerent, even at her worst, but her indifferent neglect had been just as damaging. "No booze, not for a long time."

"Hey. Brenna." Samantha's hand touched hers, then held it firmly, and her eyes lit with a familiar warmth. "That's good. I'm really glad. I was scared for you. You were drinking so much. I'm really glad you were able to stop."

"Thanks. Me too." Brenna stared down at their entwined fingers, and Sammy slipped hers free.

They sat together quietly for a while, watching the small groups of women milling around them. The square was emptying now, as the Amazons prepared for their evening council.

"The queen's awake, I hear." Samantha cradled her elbows in her palms.

"Yes." Brenna rubbed her eyes. "Shann's awake. We have no earthly idea what woke her up. Or what knocked her flat in the first place."

"You care a lot about her."

"I do."

Another silence fell between them.

"I'm sorry, Sam." Brenna kept her gaze on the tall trees ringing the village. "I hope you'll forgive me someday for bringing Caster down on you and Matt. And I'm so sorry about your daughter."

Brenna lowered her head. The words were out, and she'd needed to say them, but she expected no immediate reply. She didn't receive one. Samantha sat quietly beside her, shivering in the biting air. Brenna took off her denim jacket and wrapped it around her sister's shoulders.

"So, is it okay if I stay?" Samantha asked at last.

"Oh, honey. Of course it's okay." Brenna found a smile. "Tristaine's full of women who are refugees from the City. You can make a home here. I'll help you. Lots of us will help."

"All right. Thanks." A smile ghosted across Samantha's face.

Brenna turned as she heard the distinctive, clopping gait of a particular mountain mustang.

Jess cantered into the square, scanning the women around her, then finding Brenna. She slid from Bracken's back in one smooth motion and walked toward them. Brenna drank in the sight of Jess's wild, dark hair blowing around the planes of her face, the breadth of her shoulders, that easy, graceful step, and fell in love all over again.

She jumped from the low rock wall, met Jess midstride, and wrapped her arms around her neck with a grateful sigh.

"Where's yer coat?" Jess growled into her hair.

"I'm warm enough," Brenna mumbled. "Just don't let go."

"Never will."

Brenna finally released her and gazed up into Jess's eyes, which sparkled with warmth. "Damn. My girlfriend is such a hunk."

Jess's eyebrow arched. "A hunk, am I now?" She looked past Brenna and saw Samantha lift herself off the wall. "How's the young one, Bren?"

"Better," Brenna murmured. "We have to talk, but it can wait until after the assembly."

Jess nodded and turned to include Samantha as she joined them. "Hello, lass. Good to see you up and about."

"Hi." Samantha smiled at Jess shyly. "I guess there's big doings tonight?"

"Aye, a gathering of our clan. A good chance to see Tristaine in full force, if you're up to it."

"I am. Should I just wait here, or—?"

"Nope, nope." Brenna took her sister in one arm and Jess in the other. "We're going home. You haven't seen our cabin yet, Sammy, and Jess hasn't eaten since dawn. I'll rustle us up some dinner before the council."

"You're going to *cook*?" Samantha asked.

Brenna saw her and Jess exchange dismayed looks.

"I'm going to heat up that stew Aria made for us," Brenna corrected, leading them into the trees toward their lodge. "And if there are any more comments on my cooking prowess, I will put both of you *in* a stew to prove myself."

CHAPTER SEVEN

Vicar and Hakan carried their queen, seated on their crossed wrists, from the healing lodge to the village square. Shann was displeased, but managed to maintain her regal posture. No easy task, while being bodily handled by two Amazon warriors, however carefully. "It's never too late to introduce state executions, Jesstin."

"An idle threat, lady." Jess clasped Brenna's hand as they walked down the torchlit path. "You need me to housebreak those two barbarians carting you around."

"I do not require *carting*."

"You're still pale, Shann." Brenna threw a sympathetic look over her shoulder. "When you stop looking like cottage cheese in a crown, I'll let you cart yourself."

"Time was," Hakan drawled to Vicar, "many a wench in Tristaine would give their hallowed hymens to perch where our lady now rides. How low we studly have fallen, adanin."

"Speak for yourself, horse breath," Vicar muttered. "They still line up for me."

"I intended no offense to my brawny escorts." Shann draped her arms around their necks, regal even seated on a human throne. "Samantha?"

Sammy walked at the edge of their group, her eyes downcast. She looked surprised Shann remembered her name. "Yes, ma'am?"

"Little sister, you might have many questions after this

evening's council. Sleep on them, then seek me out tomorrow, and we'll have a nice talk."

Brenna smiled and felt Jess squeeze her hand. They were both remembering a similar invitation extended long ago by Tristaine's queen to another scared exile from the City. The "nice talks" Brenna shared with Shann had been lengthy and far-ranging, and had founded her knowledge of her new clan.

"Thanks, your...majesty." Sammy paused when Vicar snickered, and Shann rapped her smartly on the head. "I already have lots of questions."

I hope we'll have answers, Brenna thought as they entered the center of the village.

They walked into the breathing essence of Tristaine, rows upon rows of Amazons crowded into the circular clearing, awaiting their queen. The odd stillness in the midst of a gathering of nearly six hundred women struck Brenna immediately. In spite of the circumstances, Brenna felt a pleasant déjà vu as she watched Sammy absorb her first real look at her new family. Her sister's slack-jawed wonder resonated with her own memories of meeting these women, of all colors and ages, living for one purpose—to preserve the freedom and rich cultural heritage granted them by a benevolent goddess.

The square was softly illuminated by dozens of torches, and they paused in the shadows outside the reach of their golden light.

"Put me down."

It was not a request, and Vicar and Hakan obeyed at once, lowering Shann with care and supporting her as she stood erect between them.

"Brenna, you and Samantha stand within my sight, please." Shann smoothed her robe with her hands, breathing deeply. "Jesstin, be ready with our clan's sacred weapon."

Without further comment, the queen walked toward the light of the square. Jess nudged Brenna, who caught Sammy's hand and guided her quickly into the rows of seated Amazons. She saw Kyla's wave, and they joined her and Dana near the front of the assembly.

Shann emerged into the light, and the troubled silence that held the square lifted as a stir moved through the clan. Several voices called to her, and Brenna felt Sammy jerk in surprise as a musical ululation rose in waves around them, a spontaneous chorus of relief and greeting.

The queen returned their homage with a fond smile as she reached the center of the gathering and stood waiting for silence, her hands clasped behind her. It was a rather long wait, and Brenna watched Shann with something like wonder. It seemed impossible this woman had been all but comatose twenty hours ago. Her posture was relaxed, her shoulders squared, with no hint of either tension or weakness. She studied her women with alert warmth, as if she were memorizing each face.

Brenna folded her arms against the cold, uneasily aware of the stone altar behind Shann and to her left. She noted Jess had posted Hakan and Vicar between the queen and that sinister block, and she was grateful for her lover's protective instinct.

"Tristaine summons all her power tonight, adanin." Shann finally had to speak to silence the last of the ovation. "See our strength in the faces of the women beside you, and feel it in the warmth of our numbers. No force on this planet can sever the bond that unites our clan."

Shann spoke the words as simple and essential truth, and Brenna felt them deep in her gut. The square was silent now, intent on the slender figure at its center.

"Amazons have long shed dear blood to preserve the lands they called home. Our refuge in these high mountains has already cost Tristaine a strong and valiant heart. Sirius stands tonight with Kimba in the immortal guild of our clan's lost warriors."

An almost soundless sigh passed over the gathering, its sibilance whispering Sirius's name.

Samantha tugged Brenna's sleeve. "Who's Kimba?" she asked softly.

Dana answered, still riveted on Shann. "One of the Seven Sisters, the founders of Tristaine. She started our guild. She's like our alpha warrior."

Brenna and Kyla exchanged startled glances behind Dana's back, and Kyla gave her shoulder an approving pat.

"All we know of our enemy now is this," Shann continued. "Its power lies beyond the scope of our mortal plane. In order to fight it we look for passages between worlds—"

"Lady." A thin figure rose from the ranks of the seated Amazons, and an uneasy murmur went through them. A few hisses of disapproval were heard. Speaking during a full clan council was welcome, but never during the queen's address, and interrupting Shann outright was all but unheard of. Brenna craned her neck to see Wedan, one of the guild of weavers, a spare and fierce woman known for her strong will.

"I've seen Sirius, what's left of her." Wedan's tone was respectful, but her eyes on Shann were flinty. "No mere specter did that much damage. Why are we off chasing ghosts when Artemis knows Tristaine has enough enemies of flesh and blood? Why aren't our warriors scouting beyond this mesa, hunting down our prey instead of huddling here, waiting for them to come to us?"

"Wedan, your fat mouth runs away with your manners." Sarah rose from her stool stiffly, glowering at the other woman. "Close your yap and let our lady speak."

"Thank you, grandmother, for your most courtly defense." Shann smiled, and Brenna felt the tension in the women around her ease a notch. "Our sister Wedan has voiced doubts that might be shared by others among us. I offer any such concern this assurance."

Her eyes sought out Jess, who stood in the shadows. She walked into the light of the square, carrying an object draped in black silk balanced in her hands.

"We take our stand on this mesa, sisters, because the force that threatens us is here." Shann's voice rang through the square. "Before the sun rises, we'll know more about the corporeal nature of our adversary. But the blood sacrifice of Sirius has already taught us our enemy can take lethal form. Our warriors are stationed exactly where we need them, should this come to a worldly battle."

"Why don't we all just leave this place?" Samantha whispered to Brenna. "If the mesa's so dangerous—"

"Winter's coming, Sammy." Brenna looked up into the star-studded sky. Heavy cloud cover would block out their light before many weeks passed. "Imagine trying to find shelter for all these women and kids in a blizzard."

"We drowned our last village, Samantha, to keep it out of an enemy's hands." Kyla hesitated, and Brenna knew she was remembering the deep mountain lake that cloistered Camryn's bones. "We won't lose this one without a fight."

Jess reached Shann and extended the silk-shrouded form toward her. The muscles in her forearms stood out clearly, telling Brenna how heavy this object was. Shann lifted the silk covering in one graceful motion and draped it over Jess's arm. Another sigh moved through the Amazons as they saw the ebony labrys balanced in Jess's hands.

"Dyan," Kyla whispered. "That was hers. A gift from the guild of warriors when she took their command." Brenna saw Dana take Kyla's hand, and Kyla allowed her to keep it.

Jess's lips moved, but Brenna couldn't hear what she said to Shann, who replied briefly, then wrapped her hands around the two-headed axe and lifted it with apparent ease. Shann turned and stepped closer to the women watching her, the torchlight striking off the wickedly honed curved blades.

Her knuckles were white around the short-handled hilt, but Brenna could read no other sign of strain in her carriage.

"Amazons are not known for coddling bullies." Shann's smile had changed. It held steel now. It was almost predatory, and Brenna remembered this was a queen of warrior women and a seasoned fighter herself. "In the end, that's all our enemy is. It hides behind cheap spells and sneak attacks. And if it dreams to find Tristaine an easy conquest, we will offer it a grim awakening."

Shann turned and carried the labrys toward the altar. Vicar threw Jess a questioning glance, but stepped aside to let her move behind the sinister stone. Both Dana and Kyla half-rose in alarm, but Brenna gripped Dana's arm and pulled her down.

You and Samantha stand within my sight. Brenna heard Shann's words whisper through her mind again, and she grasped Sammy's hand and rose, taking her sister with her. Sammy squeaked in surprise, and Brenna shook her head slightly, her eyes on Shann.

Shann held the ebony labrys inches above the altar's surface and searched the sea of Amazons until she found Brenna. Their gaze held for a long moment, and then Shann lowered the rugged axe to the stone. The curved blades rang against the rock, a startlingly loud sound given the gentleness of their contact.

A shiver went through Brenna, but the altar offered no other outwardly dramatic effects. Shann laid her hands on the leather-wrapped hilt and waited until she and Sammy were seated.

"Adanin, we have learned this pedestal serves as a portal between worlds of the spirit." Shann brushed one hand over the glyph-marked surface of the altar. "And we have the means to open the passage connecting these worlds. Our clan's seer was gifted with a vision of a sacred plant. This night, the tea made from those blessed leaves will send our sister on a quest into the eternal."

Brenna felt the color rise in her face as the gaze of hundreds of women turned her way.

Sammy stared at her with frank wonder. "You're going *where?*" Samantha whispered.

"On a quest into the eternal," Brenna sighed. "Pay attention, Sam."

"We believe a benevolent spirit waits beyond this life to guide Tristaine's prophet." Shann looked down at the labrys, and the corner of her lips lifted in a private smile. "When the sun rises, sisters, I assure you, we'll be wiser in the ways of our enemy."

The tiers of women sat in silence, absorbing the words of their queen.

"We stand at full vigilance, adanin." Shann left the altar, and as she moved closer, Brenna noted the fine trembling in her arms. "Our warriors are well armed and primed for any physical battle. Tomorrow's rising of the Thesmophorian moon tells us events may begin to unfold more rapidly now. And we couldn't have chosen a more powerful and portentous hour to defend our clan."

Brenna started as Jess settled cross-legged beside her, her arrival as welcome as it had been silent. Her long fingers folded around Brenna's cold ones.

"This moon shines for three nights every year in celebration of the harvest," Shann continued, "and in honor of the sacred trust bonding mothers and daughters. These nights have long quickened Amazon blood and heightened the spiritual energies of our clan. Tristaine usually celebrates this festival with races, dances, and feasts."

"And serial ravishings," Aria called helpfully. This time the interruption was met with hoots of approval and lecherous nudges.

The feeling in the square was changing. Brenna sensed a new spirit growing among them. Shann's relaxed but commanding presence, and the revelation of Dyan's labrys, were empowering their clan.

"Yes, serial ravishings for the more wanton among us." Shann laughed. "But this year our revelry, carnal and otherwise, must wait. The rising of this autumn's moon finds the daughters of Artemis bracing for battle. The festivities will wait for the certain celebration of Tristaine's victory."

Shann paused as Jess let out a sharp war cry, echoed immediately by Vicar and Hakan and several others in the crowd. Brenna cocked an eyebrow at Sammy and grinned like a bandit. This was beginning to feel like a gathering of the fierce Amazons she knew and loved.

"However," Shann threw Jess a look of amused reproof, "before we close tonight's council, we'll still honor Mother Demeter's grief for her kidnapped daughter. I call upon Kyla, daughter of Viviane, to sing our Challenge."

Brenna drew in a quick breath. She and Jess both turned to Kyla, who was paling rapidly. Revered for one of the most beautiful singing voices ever to grace Tristaine, Kyla hadn't sung a note since Camryn's death. She obviously hadn't expected to be asked to do so tonight.

Shann returned her stunned look with serene patience.

Kyla's lips parted, but no words of protest emerged. The youngest daughter of Viviane was many things, Brenna thought, and a widow was only one of them. Above all she was an Amazon of Tristaine, and she did not refuse her queen. Kyla started to stand up, but her knees gave out, and she sat back down with a thump.

"I really want to hear this, Ky." Dana still held Kyla's hand, and Brenna heard a mature tenderness in her voice. "Shann's told me how much Dyan loved to hear you sing. Come on. We'll be right here." Dana pressed her fingers.

Kyla looked up at her, then turned to Brenna and Jess. Apparently finding what she needed in their faces, she rose to her feet, and a glad murmur rippled through the crowd as she met Shann at the center of the circle.

Shann took Kyla's hand in both of her own, spoke to her quietly, then smiled with loving pride and rested her lips against her pale forehead. Shann retreated to one side of the square and sat on a low stool with a shaking sigh.

Kyla faced them, her eyes downcast, and cleared her throat twice. The square was hushed, but with a different silence than the one Brenna had noted at the opening of this council. This stillness held no tension. It was filled with encouragement and warmth.

Kyla's shoulders lifted with a deep breath, and a first tentative, thready note left her lips. It drifted and faded in the chill air and was followed by another. Stronger this time, richer in melody, and then a third. Brenna felt Sammy straighten beside her and remembered how her sister relished music in all its forms.

Kyla sang, and Brenna closed her eyes as the poignant message of the Challenge spilled like gems from her lips. She remembered the last time she had heard Dyan's blood sister sing this chant, one of Brenna's first nights in Tristaine. She heard Jess's low voice again in her mind, interpreting the language of the old Amazons as she sat curled in her arms.

"Wow," Sammy whispered. She seemed spellbound by the rising beauty of Kyla's voice, soaring now to fill the square with resonant sound. Brenna watched Sam's face grow younger as she listened, grief fading from her features like the passing of a fitful dream. She leaned closer to her.

"The Mothers of Tristaine charge their daughters to protect and cherish each other." Brenna recalled Jess's translation of the lyrical, difficult tongue. "Our clan travels toward the dark night of winter. Only our shared passion can sustain us until spring's warmth returns."

Kyla's eyes closed, and her voice spiraled through a series of melancholy notes. Her tone was deeper and richer than her delicate size seemed capable of producing, and her audience listened with rapt pleasure.

A small wooden box appeared in Brenna's lap. She picked it up and studied it curiously, then nudged Jess. "What's this?" she whispered.

"A wee offerin'." Jess was watching Kyla with pride.

Brenna took off the ornate lid and set it aside, and her breasts lifted with her indrawn breath. Inside the box, nestled on a square of folded satin, lay a slender bracelet of hammered silver. Burnished to a fine sheen, it was inlaid with colorful streaks of onyx, turquoise, malachite, and red jasper.

"Jesstin," Brenna murmured. "It's beautiful." She lifted the silver band free and fit it around her wrist. The bracelet warmed at the touch of her skin, and its delicate design shimmered in the torchlight.

"You've been with us a full year, adonai." Jess slid an arm around Brenna's waist. "You walked into Tristaine for the first time under the light of Demeter's harvest moon."

"It matches this." Brenna fingered the turquoise pendant that lay in the hollow of Jess's throat. "Ah, honey. Thank you so much. I love you remembering the night I came to the village."

"I'm honoring all the nights since. You've changed my life, Brenna." Jess touched her face. "You've given me such happiness. Thank you, adonai." She lowered her head, and their lips met in a long, brushing caress.

The complete silence that greeted the last chiming notes of Kyla's Challenge brought them out of their haze. They sat up as cheers burst around them, and Brenna huffed her damp bangs off her forehead. They joined in Kyla's warm ovation, rising with their sisters to celebrate this healing.

CHAPTER EIGHT

T he village square seemed hauntingly empty to Brenna now, hours after the last of their sisters had drifted to their home lodges. The assembly had ended on a warm and vibrant note with Kyla's song, and this midnight stillness felt barren by comparison. The square itself seemed larger, its far reaches cloaked in deep shadows, and the star-swept sky above them was an implacable immensity.

In her brief tenure in the clan, Dana had mastered the art of fire building, and she had a bonfire crackling in the rock pit near the altar. Kyla sat on a low bench nearby, warming her hands by the flames. Her head was inclined toward Sarah, who sat beside her, drawing on her pipe. The old woman caught Brenna's eye and winked before resuming her story.

"Lady," Jess called. "I need a word."

"Jess," Brenna sighed.

"No, Bren." Jess covered the hand Brenna laid on her arm with her own. "This needs to be said."

Shann was deep in conference with Aria, who tended a boiling kettle. Aria wafted the fragrant steam swirling from the pot's interior to her face with a twirl of her wrist, the image of a voluptuous elder witch. Shann lifted a hand to acknowledge Jess, but her fingers spun a request for patience. She whispered a last word to Aria, then joined Brenna and Jess.

"What is it, Jesstin?" Shann looked harried. She brushed a tumbling lock of hair off her forehead, her cheeks flushed by the heat of the fire. "We're nearly ready. Brenna, we can only estimate the intensity of this brew by fragrance and color. But I promise you, it's the mildest dose discernible."

"My lady queen." Jess reached for Shann's hand and held it until she looked up into her eyes. "You know I trust you with my whole heart. Hear me now."

The impatience faded from Shann's features. "I'm listening, Jess."

"You and Brenna believe Dyan waits for her on the far side of the veil." Jess's tone was respectful. "But the blood of Sirius is still fresh on our hands, Shann. We don't know who or what else Brenna might find there."

"True enough, Jesstin." Shann looked at Brenna with shadowed eyes. "I understand all too well the risks we're asking your adonai to face."

"We can mitigate them. Send me with her, lady."

"Dear one." Shann laid her hand on Jess's cheek. "We can't know what effect this tea would have on an Amazon with no natural psychic shields. Brenna is virtually the only woman among us with some assurance of safe travel. Believe me, I would go in our sister's place myself if I could."

"Like Brenna, I accept the risks of this journey." Jess took Shann's hands in her own. "And I'll look to her for protection, when it comes to phantoms. All I ask is your leave to safeguard my wife against more visceral enemies."

"Brenna is more than your wife to Tristaine, Jesstin," Shann said gently.

"Of course she is." Jess glanced at Brenna, and even through her urgency there was warm pride in her eyes. "As much as I love Brenna, lady, it's not her protection alone that drives me. I seek this honor for the sake of our clan as well. If Tristaine loses her only prophet, we lose our connection to divine help."

"I can't allow it, Jess." Shann squeezed Jess's hands. "This sacred plant might even prove poisonous to one outside the guild of seers, and the life of the leader of our warriors is also precious to Tristaine. We must let Brenna make this journey alone."

"Excuse me." Brenna tapped her way politely in between Jess and Shann. "As the endangered party, may I add to this discussion?"

She noted Jess had the grace to flush. "Of course, lass."

"Jesstin." Brenna stepped closer to her. "I know you trust me with your life. You have yet to learn to trust me with the welfare of our clan."

"Ah, Bren." Jess sounded dismayed. "Of course I trust you. I never meant—"

"Hush, then." Brenna laid her fingers against Jess's lips. "Just listen a minute." She extended her arm and showed her the silver bracelet adorning her wrist. "I earned my year in Tristaine, Jess, every day of it. I've fought in our battles, and tended our wounded, and buried our dead. I climbed over a mountain range with every other woman in the tribe to reach this mesa. True?"

"True, Brenna."

"Every Amazon in Tristaine is willing to defend her sisters with her life." Brenna poked Jess's chest to emphasize her point, but then softened her hand against her breast. "That's what you told me, one night in the Clinic when you were so homesick for these women I was afraid your heart might stop."

Brenna measured the steady pulse beneath her palm, willing Jess to absorb understanding through the pores of her skin. A hundred faces flickered through her mind, sisters she had met and grown to love, only because of this one obstinate Amazon. "This is my clan now too, adonai. Tristaine took me in, and I've found family here. I've earned the right to protect my sisters." She cradled Jess's face in her hands. "I'm sorry, love, but where I'm going tonight, you can't follow. You have to let me walk by my own light."

The square was quiet, save for the snapping of the fire, until Sarah rose from her bench with a dry cackle. "Madlady's moon, Shann. To the very word, you gave that speech to Dyan, the night before your first battle."

"I remember, grandmother." Shann cupped the back of Brenna's neck and smiled at Jess. "It's the hardest work our Mothers ask of us, Jesstin, risking the women we love in order to preserve the clan we all cherish. I'm afraid it never gets easier, adanin."

Jess released a sigh as bleak as a wind-swept glacier. "I hear you, lady."

Brenna stood on her toes and brushed a swift kiss on Jess's cheek.

"Ladies?" Aria wrapped a cloth around the kettle's handle and lifted it off the fire. "I'm afraid it's teatime in Tristaine."

One by one the women rose and drifted toward the stone altar. Brenna shivered and turned back to Jess, who lowered her head until their foreheads met. They leaned lightly against each other, the swells of Brenna's breasts cushioning Jess's firm ones. It was one of their favorite ways of touching, and they relaxed in the unique and sensual comfort of this quiet blending of their bodies.

"Okay," Brenna whispered, closing her eyes, "so after the I-am-much-woman speech, I can still tell you I'm scared witless, right?"

Jess's arms were strong and warm around her. "You'd be daft not to be, Bren."

"You'll stay close."

"Hell's fury can't move me."

Brenna opened her eyes and filled her lungs with cold air. Then she let go of Jess and walked to the altar.

Dana and Kyla stepped apart to admit her to the circle of women around the black stone, and Kyla gripped Brenna's hand with chilly fingers as she passed. Dana gave her shoulder an awkward pat. Brenna offered them what she hoped was a reassuring smile, but her teeth were chattering, and the effect was probably a bit macabre.

"Shanendra wouldn't let me add anything, Brenna." Aria tisked as she poured the steaming amber liquid from the kettle into a silver cup resting on the altar's surface. "Not one drop of honey, not one sprig of mint—"

"Peace, Aria, you've done well." Shann helped her lower the kettle to a nearby rock. She turned to Brenna and took her hands. "Are you ready, adanin?"

"I need a drink." Brenna tried to smile. "Something with a little kick. I guess this brew will have to do." She felt a tremor in Shann's hands and pressed them gently. "I'm ready, lady."

"Safe journey, little sister." Shann kissed her forehead. "Come home to us soon."

Brenna felt the altar lurking behind her like a living presence. The craggy stone block still pulsed with a banked power. It carried as much sinister menace as the granite sculpture near the cemetery had evoked poignant grief. Brenna didn't let herself see the sigils carved into its surface. Instead, she focused on the leather-hilted labrys still resting in its center.

She lifted the gleaming silver cup and cradled it in her palms, the heat emanating through the metal shocking her cold fingers. She held it beneath her nose, her eyes crinkling at the sharp fragrance rising with the steam. The pungent tea carried a faint licorice scent, which seemed a hopeful sign.

The faces around Brenna were a study in watchful tension. The firelight reached them only faintly this close to the altar, and their features were washed in soft reddish light. Sarah stood motionless, her shawl wrapped around her bony shoulders, betraying her worry only through her rapid draws on her pipe. Aria's beautiful features held no trace of humor, and Kyla and Dana were both visibly pale. Brenna met Shann's shadowed gaze, then reached for Jess's hand.

To her own surprise, Brenna murmured a brief prayer before she drank. She wasn't specific about who she was praying to. Just those phantom women every Amazon called on in times of need, with a child's pure faith that her Mothers will hear her.

The thin liquid flooded Brenna's mouth with heat and a taste more bitter than she'd expected, and her throat almost closed. She swallowed hard, then drained the cup in three determined gulps.

Kyla gasped somewhere behind her. "Is she supposed to bolt it like that, lady?"

"We don't know how quickly this tea might act, Ky." Shann took the cup from Brenna's hand and studied her face closely. "How are you, Blades?"

"Fine, thanks. How are you?" Brenna realized she was squeezing Jess's hand with painful force and made herself relax her grip. She opened her eyes, and the sculpted lines of Jess's face swam into focus. Or almost. She was starting to sparkle a bit around the edges. A mild wave of dizziness went through Brenna. "Maybe I should lie down."

There was a flurry of movement around her, and careful hands helped her sit on the black altar. Jess lifted her legs, and Shann took Brenna's shoulders and eased her down until she was lying flat.

"*Jeeze,* this thing is cold," she hissed. A certain chill might be expected from a stone block, but the cold seeping into Brenna from its dense depths seemed almost arctic. She shifted and quickly gave up finding any semblance of comfort on the craggy rock.

"This part just kills me." Dana's voice reached her faintly. "She looks like some virgin sacrifice laid out on this thing. Plus, as far as we know, this altar might eat people. Wouldn't a warm cabin have been just as good for this ritual?"

"This altar is our doorway, Dana." Shann's hand was warm on Brenna's hair. "Everything is centered here."

"Bren."

She opened her eyes. Jess stood close beside the altar, holding the labrys. The rising moon loomed behind her, outlining her muscular form in silver light. Brenna opened her hands and accepted the revered weapon, resting its curved blades over her breasts and holding the short hilt near her waist. Its solid weight was comforting, an anchor holding down the frenzied fireflies in her belly.

"Just breathe slowly, Brenna." Shann's fingers moved through her hair.

She was starting to feel decidedly odd. A prickly lightness filled her stomach and spread up into her chest.

"I'm here, Bren." Jess's large hand covered her own.

She felt her body grow weightless, as if she were evaporating into an insubstantial mist, and something cell-deep in Brenna rebelled at this alien state. She tightened hard, her back arching against the stone, then felt a horrific sensation of melting down into the altar itself, vanishing into that malign black bulk.

"Relax, dear one." Shann's breath brushed her forehead. "It's all right, Brenna. You know what to do. Trust your sight."

Brenna focused on the midnight heavens above her, each pinpoint of light a crisp pinwheel against the velvet sky. Seven particular stars formed a firmament that flickered brightest and drew her toward them like a celestial tide calling its lost children home.

Abruptly the Seven Sisters sparked and telescoped into rushing streaks of light, and Brenna felt herself soaring upward, twisting in gentle spirals of warm wind.

❖

Lush grass tickled her ankles—thick, cool, and a dazzling deep green.

Brenna blinked and raised her head.

The sun-drenched light that flooded the clearing struck her first, startling after the soft mist of the mesa. Startling, too, that in the village square it was cresting midnight, and here—wherever "here" was—it seemed to be high noon.

She stood in an open, grassy space at the edge of a thick forest, beneath a cloudless sky saturated with rich blue. It took Brenna a moment to realize the heavy weight in her hands was the ebony labrys, and she gripped its hilt gratefully.

Brenna breathed in a chestful of the sweetest air ever to grace a human lung and let Jess's training take over. She turned in a tight circle, surveying the terrain, the two-headed axe held ready for a quick defense. She was alone, that much was obvious, and no immediate threat set off her internal alarms. Her pounding heart began to ease to a more comfortable rhythm.

She knew this place. Perhaps only in dreams, but its beauty resonated in Brenna's memory. She'd stood on this goddess-graced ground before.

Brenna completed her circle and let out an abrupt yelp of dismay. She was perched at the edge of a virtual cliff. The earth dropped off abruptly only inches from her boots. Brenna leaned forward to trace the wall's sheer descent to a rocky floor a good two thousand feet below, then straightened quickly.

"Great, heights will still scare the crap out of me in heaven," Brenna muttered, her hand to her breast.

"Amazons need courage in all their lives."

A ragged gasp burst from Brenna, and she whirled, the double-bladed axe swinging in a clumsy circle before her. Unaccustomed to its weight, she nearly lost her footing, but managed to regain it with an unlovely lurch.

The giant of her vision towered over her. She wasn't glowing anymore, but she was still a giant, and now her handsome features were crystal clear. The dark woman easily topped nine feet, not counting her boots. The muscles of her crossed arms stood out in stark relief, and her entire being emanated a sinewy strength. Eyes black as obsidian regarded Brenna quizzically.

"You're Dy..." Brenna's words died in her throat. "You couldn't be."

She remembered and treasured Jess's vivid description of Shann's adonai. Though they shared a common mother, Dyan had rough features that carried none of Kyla's delicate beauty. Ravishing in the strength of her spirit, in life Dyan had been short, broad as a barn, freckled, and plain as dirt. The black-haired colossus before her was stunning.

She unfolded her arms and crooked two fingers at Brenna. "Ye hold what's mine." The malted brogue clearly echoed the voice that had called to her at the river.

Brenna felt the labrys vibrate in her hands. It lifted abruptly out of her grasp and sailed through the air in a pure arc to its true owner. The woman caught the weapon with one lazy snap of a wrist, and the labrys was transformed by her touch. The double-bladed head shimmered, then transformed from pitted steel to some flawless black metal that sparked sunlight off its glossy surface. The hilt grew longer and became a dark, gleaming rosewood, balanced effortlessly in the warrior's powerful grip.

A very human fondness flickered across her beautiful features as her fingers flexed around the axe's hilt. She sent the curved blades in a tight, whistling circle around her head so fast Brenna could hardly follow the motion, the wicked edges slicing a note of music out of the clear air. The labrys snapped neatly into the leather sheath strapped across her broad back.

Brenna saw the sun spark off the simple silver ring on the giant's third finger. It was identical to the band Shann wore. Unlike the labrys, this symbol of their bond was unchanged from its earthly form, and Brenna understood that this crude ring was already perfection.

"Dyan," she whispered.

Dyan grinned, and now Brenna could see her little sister in her. There was a gamin quality in that smile that was all Kyla.

"Short, was I now?"

"N-not anymore," Brenna admitted. "Can I ask where we are?"

"You've not traveled far in one sense, lass." Dyan's voice rang like a deep bell. She set her hands on her hips and nodded toward the dense forest. "We stand at the edge of the mesa this generation of Tristaine calls home."

"We do?" Brenna asked politely. She glanced over her shoulder and shuddered at the sheer drop behind her. The mesa she knew didn't involve towering cliffs.

"We haven't much time, Brenna, so listen well." Dyan lowered herself slowly to one knee next to her, and Brenna had a vivid memory of her doing so, with equal care, in her vision. Now she only had to crane her neck slightly to look into her dark eyes.

"The demon who plagues Tristaine was an Amazon queen. And a powerful sorceress. She ruled this mesa three hundred years ago. And she destroyed her own clan. Made them blood sacrifices to the dark gods to win immortality for her poxed soul."

Brenna felt that appalling betrayal deep in her gut and heard it echoed in the revulsion in Dyan's rich voice.

"Her undead spirit slaughtered a second Amazon tribe who inhabited this mesa a century later. And she means to make the adanin of Tristaine her next victims."

"Wait a minute." A frisson of fear coursed down Brenna's back. She heard Kyla's voice in her mind, at the storyfire three nights ago, telling the chilling ghost story that held the clan rapt. *"Are we talking about that legend? That demon queen who sucks the souls out of Amazons? Botesh?"*

"Botesh," Dyan confirmed *"The name means 'shame' in a dozen languages. She's more than legend, girl. If she enslaves the spirits of a third Amazon clan, she'll fill her unholy pact with her dark masters. She'll regain human form, with all the powers of her sorcery intact. And that twisted canker will be as immortal as the gods themselves."*

"That's not going to happen." Rage shook Brenna, drowning her fear, and her palms itched for a weapon. The warrior in her was rising fast. *"Tell us what to do, Dyan."*

Dyan's eyes glinted. *"Give this message to m'lady, Brenna. Tristaine's greatest warriors can't stop Botesh. Only an Amazon queen, an equally powerful light matched to her darkness, can vanquish this evil. But Shann must not face her alone."*

Her huge hand rested gently on Brenna's shoulder. *"Tell her she must call on the Maiden, the Mother, and the Crone. Their blended powers are Tristaine's only hope. Shanendra will ken my meaning."*

"I sure hope so," Brenna whispered. *"You couldn't possibly be any more specific, though? In case she has any questions?"*

"Ha. Think I'm vague?" Dyan snorted and got to her feet, towering over Brenna again. *"Our Mothers don't speak much more clearly on this plane, lass. Try getting a straight answer out of those seven stubborn..."*

Dyan looked to the trees as a faint, trilling whistle reached them.

Brenna's mouth was open to ask the next of six dozen essential questions, but it snapped shut again as she recognized that particular pattern of whistled notes.

The sound came from the dense trees bordering the small meadow. Brenna's heart beat faster, and she looked at Dyan. The immense warrior's chiseled face softened, and she nodded.

Brenna stepped through the lush grass toward the forest's edge, stooping to peer through the thick branches. The swirling whistle came again, and she stopped. She saw her now. A tall, slim young warrior with chestnut hair, standing on a far-distant ridge, strong and vibrant with life.

Camryn was too far away to allow speech, and Brenna didn't attempt it. They regarded each other across the distance, both grinning like fools. A joyful laugh rose from Brenna's throat, and she gave in to the irresistible, childlike urge to wave her arm in huge arcs in greeting. Cam lifted her hand in return, laughing too.

"She can't come closer, lass." Dyan's low voice sounded in her mind. "She's still learning the lay of the land."

Brenna nodded, drinking in every detail of the distant figure. Camryn's hand moved over her chest, and her long fingers twirled in an intricate design. Brenna shouldn't have been able to see the motion clearly at this distance, but she followed it easily, and it imprinted on her heart.

Brenna raised her hand in acknowledgement and caught the flash of Camryn's grin. The young warrior stood a moment longer, relaxed and easy in a body that had been gangly and restless on earth. Then she turned and walked back into the surrounding trees.

Brenna stared at the empty ridge, her fingers brushing the base of her throat.

Dyan waited for her at the edge of the cliff. They stood side by side, looking out over a vista of mountains and valleys more crisp and beautiful than any view offered on Brenna's mesa.

"You need to go back, adanin."

Brenna murmured agreement. "Is there anything else I should tell them?"

"Aye. Botesh's power peaks with tomorrow's dawn of Demeter's moon. Expect her attack at nightfall. And don't drop your guard. If the she-ghoul survives the first night, she'll return the second."

"I understand." Brenna thought that might be overstating it, but at least she understood what to tell Shann and Jess. "Is that all?"

Dyan's hand rose to her breast, and her fingers moved in the same twirling motion Camryn's had, with a slight variation at the end. "Tell m' lady I hear her. Each and every night."

Brenna swallowed hard. "I will, Dyan."

Dyan straightened and looked down at Brenna from her dizzying height. "Do you trust me, Brenna?"

"Yes, I do." She didn't have to think about it.

"Then trust your sight." Dyan put a large hand in the small of Brenna's back and pushed her off the cliff.

❖

At first she just plummeted, her arms pinwheeling helplessly, her ragged scream sucked back into her throat by the wind. Brenna's lifelong nightmares crystallized in those few seconds of stark terror. And then she was lifted.

Her spirit changed and soared, a painless transformation that sent her reeling high into the cloudless, sunlit heavens. She turned and stretched in the warm winds, the terrain spinning with her, her fear giving way to exhilaration. Jesstin, *she yelled in her mind,* see me now!

Only now, high above the earth, could Brenna realize the truth of Dyan's words. This was *Tristaine's mesa, albeit larger and more spectacularly beautiful than the one Shann's*

Amazons inhabited. She could see the ring of towering trees outlining its perimeter and stopped in her headlong flight, hovering over the mesa's center.

Small details registered: the tiny blocks of lodges and cabins that dotted the Amazon village, the lush conifers growing thickly among them. But Brenna was struck by an amazing symmetry evident only at this height.

The outer ring of trees wasn't just regular; it was perfect, forming a wide and solid circle around the mesa's surface. And several hundred yards in, another concise circle of trees grew, forming an inner ring. There was an obvious gap—an empty space, forested only by shrubs and smaller trees, where a third circle should be. And there, in the exact geometric center of these natural rings, Brenna saw the sinister black shape of the altar.

The target glyph, the image of the bull's-eye, its grooves sizzling with Sirius's blood. The sigil carved onto the altar was replicated almost perfectly on the mesa's surface. It lacked only the third, innermost ring.

And then Brenna was falling again, no, diving. There was no sense of helplessness now, just a desperate urgency to get home to her clan. She streaked down toward the altar, fixing her furious gaze on its malignant form, seeing it grow larger as if rising to meet her attack.

❖

"She'll be with us soon, Jesstin."

Shann's voice, immensely weary but rich with relief. Brenna could feel her fingers stroking her hair again and Jess's firm grip on her hand.

"Hoo," Brenna whispered.

"Brenna." Jess's breath warmed her brow. Brenna could feel the faint trembling in her fingers.

She opened her eyes, and the first thing she saw was

the blurred montage, high overhead, of the Seven Sisters. Then Jess's tense features swam into focus, filling her sky, and Brenna realized that cherished gaze was all she would ever need of heaven.

"Get me off this thing," she mumbled, and Jess's arms slid under her shoulders and knees at once and lifted her gently from the altar.

"Here, Jesstin, near the fire." Shann motioned to Dana, who snapped out a warm fur and spread it close to the crackling flames.

Rather than lay Brenna on the blanket, Jess settled cross-legged onto it herself and cradled her in her lap. Brenna was starting to shiver from the night's cold now and welcomed the warmth of the fire, but the strong arms supporting her offered more exquisite comfort.

She heard the stirring of cloaks and robes as Shann and the others gathered around them. The relief of the breathing presence of her sisters was so great Brenna felt faint with it. Shann knelt in front of her and lifted her hand.

"How are you, little sister?"

"Lady," Brenna began, "please, please, please tell me you know three women called the Maiden, the Mother, and the Crone."

A quicksilver array of emotions passed over Shann's expressive features. She masked her fear almost at once, but Brenna saw it clearly.

CHAPTER NINE

Brenna sat near the edge of the highest bluff their mesa afforded—a tame drop-off, compared to its counterpoint in the spirit world. The tree she leaned against was one of those towering conifers that formed the outer ring encircling their village.

She rested her head against the soft moss cushioning the trunk of the tree and allotted herself exactly thirty seconds of closed eyes and relaxed vigilance. If Botesh and her minions chose to attack in those thirty seconds, she was prepared to accept full blame.

The sun was an hour from setting. They had until nightfall, Dyan had said. Shann seemed to accept this assurance, and the rest of her lost adonai's instruction, as literal truth. She had told them she understood who this mysterious Crone, Mother, and Maiden were, and how they could help Tristaine. Beyond that, Shann declined to elaborate.

Snugging the collar of her jacket closer around her throat, Brenna shivered in the breeze of early evening. It had been a day of frenetic activity. She had spent much of it in Tristaine's healing lodge, rolling bandages and stocking Shann's supplies to prepare for the coming battle.

Which would take what form? Brenna folded her arms, curled her legs beneath her on the rocky ground, and looked out over the twilight pasture below. Jess's warriors were braced for armed conflict. Their children and elderly were housed in fortified cabins that would be well guarded until the clan was safe. Food was stored in their harvesting bins to see them through any siege that might confine them to the mesa. They were as ready as they could be for physical battle, but it seemed there was little more they could do to raise shields against the spectral forces their enemy might command.

Shann had shepherded her women ably through all these preparations. She claimed a good night's sleep had restored her energies and brushed aside any attempt at solicitude. But throughout the day, Shann seemed to avoid being alone with Brenna and rarely met her eye. A small thing with so many urgent demands on a queen's attention, but the loss of that direct, warm gaze troubled Brenna.

Eyes still closed, she heard the outraged rustling coming up on her left.

"Great! She's asleep. We could have crossbowed your butt three times already, Brenna." It was Dana's voice.

Brenna crooked one eye open and smiled a greeting at Kyla and Samantha as they joined Dana around her moss-sheathed tree.

"And what part of Jess's order about no one traveling alone beyond the village didn't register with you?" Dana continued to crab. "You really want to bring the wrath of that big snarly adonai of yours down on your—yipe!" She broke off as an acorn bounced smartly off the top of her head.

Brenna craned her neck and watched Jess descend from her watch atop a nearby oak. She sluiced down through the branches, sinuous as a panther, moving almost soundlessly. Jumping the last ten feet, she landed lightly, with the smallest flex of her knees. Brenna made a clicking noise and smiled in wicked appreciation, and Jess winked at her.

"Make that big sneaky adonai," Dana muttered, rubbing her head.

"I take it by your presence that all's quiet in the village." Jess lifted Kyla's hand and kissed it.

"As a tomb." Kyla tousled Jess's hair. "A quiet, tense, ticking, pressurized tomb."

"The night watch is coming on, Jess." Dana shrugged the strap of a canvas bag off her shoulder and knelt to rummage through it. "I heard Siirah and Reilly ride past a minute ago. This sector is set. Aria sent up this tasty ch—this dinner for us."

"Hey, you." Brenna smiled at Samantha and patted the ground beside her. "Pull up a root."

Sammy complied, folding her coltish legs beneath her and settling between Brenna and Dana. The climb to this low ridge had done her sister good, Brenna noted. Or maybe it was the quiet ministration Sammy had received from their clan the last few days. That persistent pallor had faded a little, and her expression seemed more alert and focused.

Towering waves of terror and dread were impossible to sustain, Brenna philosophized as Dana passed thick mutton sandwiches around their circle. She often wrote her journal in her mind long before ink touched paper. She saw the tension ease from the bodies of her friends as they began to relish their collective warmth. They had all been swept up in the adrenaline-charged preparations since they were last together, and it was past time for this brief reprieve.

"So Shann really understands this whole crone-virgin thing?" Dana obviously didn't comprehend the nature of a reprieve, which in Brenna's mind meant ignoring the looming threat altogether.

Kyla sputtered, then lowered the canteen, giggling. "That's *Maiden,* you heretic. The Crone, the Mother, and the Maiden. That's covered in, what, Introduction to Amazons? The *virgin.*"

"Okay, the Crone, the Mama, and the Maid." Dana grinned. "Same difference. Did Shann say any more about who they're supposed to be?"

"Our lady keeps her own counsel." Jess chewed methodically, studying the sparse grass of the pasture below them. "She hasn't shared her thoughts with me."

That in itself was unusual, and troubling, Brenna thought. Jess served as Shann's second and had always been one of her most trusted advisors.

"Were they Amazons, these three women?" Sammy was wolfing down her dinner with obvious pleasure.

"They're three aspects of our Goddess, Samantha." Jess brushed her hands together and leaned back on one elbow. "But many other cultures share the archetype. The wise elder, the fruitful mother, the innocent girl. They are the new, full, and waning moons. Sedna, Demeter, and Persephone. The most potent ages of Woman, embodied in those three."

"Wow." Samantha swallowed the last of her sandwich. She watched Brenna closely, as if trying to read her response to all this. "I'm sorry, but I don't know anything about your religion. So I'm not sure how these three…um, aspects of your goddess figure in here. Everybody's getting ready for this big physical battle. But aren't you talking about some…spiritual war? I just don't see how swords can protect us against ghosts."

"Our battlefield was cast the night Sirius died, Samantha." Jess met Brenna's gaze, and Brenna picked up her thought effortlessly.

"I'm glad you weren't there to see her body, Sam." A sad shiver moved through Brenna. "Sirius was killed with terrible violence. It's all the proof we need that Botesh can attack us on the physical plane. That's why Jess's warriors are on full watch."

"Brenna said Sirius's slaughter was a blood sacrifice." Grief and anger melded in Kyla's voice. "It opened a door between worlds and let Botesh in."

"Doors swing both ways, Ky." Jess nudged Kyla's knee

gently with her foot. "Tristaine has her own allies in Botesh's realm. If that banshee can reach us, so can they. If Shann calls on our Goddess, her Crone, Mother, and Maiden will answer."

"But how will she call them? Please tell me it won't involve anyone stretching out on that creep-show altar again." Dana scratched her shoulder. "And how will we use them once they get here?"

"Shann will need their blended powers to face Botesh." Brenna closed her eyes, remembering. "That's what Dyan said. I asked her to be more specific about the whole blending thing, but she just said Shann would understand."

"She said she'd *ken*," Kyla murmured.

"She did." Brenna nodded.

"I can't believe you spoke to her." Kyla lifted Brenna's hand onto her knee. "You stood right in front of her, Bren."

"And she was something to see." Brenna smiled.

"Dyan was your real sister, right, Kyla?" Samantha asked. "I mean, your biological sister?"

Kyla nodded. "I only had her for a few years. We grew up in different villages, raised by separate branches of Tristaine. But I always knew Dyan existed. I heard stories about her my whole life. And I dreamed about her, even before we met. The bond between blood sisters can be so intense and so sweet. You know about that, Sammy."

Brenna felt Samantha go still beside her. She held her breath, glad she couldn't see her sister's face. Kyla pressed her hand, sending her faith.

"Yes, I do," Samantha said softly.

Brenna smiled at the ground and pressed Kyla's hand back, sending her thanks.

"So that explains why Dyan had this huge accent and you don't." Dana tossed a small pebble lightly in Kyla's direction. "You grew up in different villages."

"Aye, lassie," Kyla replied in a deep brogue. "Dyan's trrrribe was a bunch o' crrrude barbarians, who slaughtered all their 'rrr's."

"She would mean me," Jess drawled. "Dyan brought Vicar and me with her when she joined this clan, Dana."

"Jeeze." Dana scowled. "Y'all's history is complicated enough without breaking into clan offshoots. You were born in this part of Tristaine, right, Ky?"

"Yep, Camryn and Lauren and I were all homegrown." Kyla smiled at Samantha. "Lauren was Cam's blood sister. Maybe you should be taking notes."

"Good idea," Sammy sighed.

Brenna sat quietly through the relaxed banter that followed. The warmth between Dana and Kyla was palpable tonight, almost flirtatious. Their fragile bond had grown strong since Tristaine had found this mesa.

Brenna had a message for Kyla, one that might rekindle old grief, and she was reluctant to dim the new light in her sister's eyes. But they hovered on the brink of battle, and there was no promise of future council. Brenna looked at Jess to gather her courage and cleared her throat.

"I saw Camryn, Ky."

Kyla said nothing for a moment. She laid down a wedge of cheese and brushed her hands together carefully. A tremor shook her, but her eyes on Brenna were calm. "Tell me, adanin."

"She was as strong as a young horse." Warmth surged through Brenna as she remembered the spirit warrior's vibrant energy. "And grinning like a demon. She's home, Kyla. Safe in Dyan's care and thriving on her own path."

Kyla drew in a deep breath and looked at her hands folded in her lap. Her sisters waited with her. Dana sat with one elbow on a raised knee, watching Kyla with unreadable eyes.

"Did she speak?" Kyla asked finally.

Brenna nodded. "She was too far away for voices, but she sends you this."

She lifted her hand to her waist and performed the intricate twirling motion of wrist and fingers Camryn had formed on the ridge. Kyla's lips parted, and her eyes filled with tears. Then she smiled, and Brenna remembered Shann's belief that the very act of smiling through tears held the essence of healing.

Brenna felt Samantha touch her back.

"Is it okay to ask?"

Brenna waited until Kyla nodded. "Sure, Sam." She shifted so her sister could see her hands. "Amazons can communicate amazing things through hand signals." She dipped her fingers in a subtle curve. "This is the universal signal for a deep and abiding love, the bond between adonai."

"It's how we greeted each other." Kyla brushed her hand across her cheek.

"Dyan sent Shann the same message." Brenna touched Kyla's knee. "And Cam sent you this wish, Ky." She painted a gentle pattern with her fingers.

Kyla's brow furrowed. "Peace?"

"Peace." Brenna smoothed Kyla's hair off her forehead. She knew that word held realms of meaning for her, beyond the immediate fate of their clan. It was what Shann had sought since Dyan's death, and what Samantha desperately needed now. Inner peace was Camryn's unselfish wish for an end to her adonai's mourning.

"Listen." Jess was suddenly alert as a feral cat, then Brenna heard it, an urgent trumpeting of hooves over the hard-packed earth.

Siirah appeared above them, reining in her plunging roan. "Jesstin! You'd best get to the village."

Jess rose to her feet. "What's happening, Siirah?"

"No enemy has been sighted, Jess. But there's…you'd best see for yourself, adanin."

Jess whistled acknowledgement, and Siirah wheeled her horse and cantered back down the rise. "Kyla, take Samantha to the elders' cabin, then join us in the square. Dana, Brenna, with me."

"Hey, wait." Samantha touched Jess's arm. "I don't want to hide in some cabin. If Bree—if everybody's going to be out there, I want to be too. I won't get in the way."

Jess glanced at Brenna, then nodded. "Just don't make me tell you anything twice, lass."

They gathered their things quickly and moved in one close unit toward the trail leading down to the village. Brenna paused before following the others into the thick of the trees and looked over her shoulder. She had felt its weak light on her back even before turning. It was still a mild sickle, rising over the far mountain crest. The first dawn of the Thesmophorian moon.

Brenna invoked any goddesses still listening and ran swiftly after her sisters.

❖

She nearly smacked into Jess's broad back when they slid to a stop.

They stood at the head of the narrow trail, looking down a low rise to the Amazon village below. It was a cold night, and twilight had surrendered to full darkness now. The stars glittered with uncommon brilliance, and the rising moon had started to bleed its own murky light, casting Tristaine in a dull silver glow.

"What in Hera's left tit is that?" Dana stared down at the gathering of lodges.

"Fog," Jess answered rhetorically, and Brenna wrapped

her fingers around her forearm for reassurance.

Only an Amazon, who referred to mountains as hills and canyons as ditches, would consider this brackish mess *fog*. Brenna knew mountain fog now and welcomed the soft mists that graced many of their mornings. And her sense memory still carried the distinctly unpleasant chemical stench of the City's air. If this stuff was fog, it was the kind only a City could generate.

Rivers of it drifted like curdled streams of liquid cheese through the cabins and trees below. It emitted a scent almost discernable from this distance, but it was no odor Brenna recognized, more a malign memory of mildew.

"This is Botesh's herald, adanin." Kyla drew in a long breath. "Remember the legend. The coming of the demon is signaled by a thick, strange mist."

"Thick, strange, check." Dana turned to Jess for instructions, but closed her mouth at the grim light in her eyes. Jess slipped the leather notch from her belt to free her sword, and Brenna felt a thrill of pride. She hadn't seen Jesstin of Tristaine in full battle mode for three seasons, and the sight of her brought Dyan's spectral grandeur to mind.

"Our wait's over." Jess's upper lip curled. "We've a bully to spank." She spun and jumped a dozen feet down the hill, and they exploded after her.

Dana's war cry, a damn fine one for a debut, rattled the trees. Brenna reached back and touched Sammy's chest as they ran, making sure she stayed close.

There was a definite stirring in the village, the ignition of a strategy set carefully in place. They passed running women, efficient bands of three and four, bound for sentry posts and defense positions. Voices shouted to each other, not in panic, but in a crisp cadence acknowledging orders. Shann had prepared her women well.

Brenna wanted to keep running. She had the wind to circle

the mesa a dozen times. The adrenaline coursing through her might be enough to boost her to another flight above it. Some of the hot joy that ignited Jess's expressive features heated Brenna's blood as well, an alien but welcome energy. A healer to her core, she had never felt less conflicted going into a fight. Their enemy was anathema to generations of Amazons, and her reign would end here.

"Vicar!" Jess reached up and snatched the bridle of her cousin's horse as she reined in beside them. "Where's our lady?"

"Shann awaits you in the square, Jesstin. We're ready. I join Hakan on the west flank."

Jess clapped her horse's rump in reply, and Vicar cantered off into the trees.

Brenna sensed Jess's urgency to reach Shann, and she more than shared it. The five women moved as quickly as they could toward the square. The odious fog curling about their knees made for uneasy footing.

They found Shann easily. Closely guarded by a small phalanx of warriors, she waited near the roaring bonfire that cast red shadows across the stone altar. She pushed back the hood of her elegant winter robe and smiled when she sighted them.

"Thank you, adanin," Shann touched the back of one of the warriors guarding her. "My family is here now. Please go see to the safety of yours."

Jess issued quiet orders to two of the Amazons as they passed, then nodded respectfully to Shann. "Lady, our lines are well set."

"Of course they are, Jesstin. Nicely done." Shann rose on her toes to kiss Jess's cheek. She looked exhausted to Brenna, but she still managed to exude an unmistakable aura of regality. "Sisters, join me, please."

They moved with Shann to the altar and grouped loosely

around it. Tristaine's labrys rested on the black stone's surface, and Brenna brushed her fingers across one rough blade, a comforting genuflection.

"As our warriors take up arms on their field of battle, we make our stand here." Shann's voice was low, but it reached Brenna clearly. "Call on your Mothers, dear ones, and prepare yourselves for whatever comes."

The square was quieting around them as the last Amazons reached their assigned stations. The slick fog swirled wetly around their knees, and Brenna had to resist the persistent urge to scrub her feet against her calves.

Sammy stepped closer to Brenna. "Who said that?" she whispered.

Brenna looked at her, puzzled.

"Lady? Shann?" Dana's voice was hushed. "Sorry, but shouldn't we be calling in our allies? The Crone and the Mother and the Maiden?"

"They're here, Dana." Shann looked grim. "But they can't materialize until Botesh herself enters this plane."

Brenna touched her sister's wrist. "Who said what, Sammy?"

J'heika, rise.

Brenna froze.

"Who said *that*?" Sammy frowned. "And who's J'heika?"

Brenna couldn't move. Jess threw her a quick look, her expression darkening. She drew her sword.

And the dead came to life around them.

❖

A sinister growl filled the air, like the rending of snarled roots from blasted earth.

"Shann?" Brenna's throat was dry as ash. "She's coming."

Strident whistles broke out almost simultaneously from three different directions. Brenna's blood chilled as she recognized the identical signals of imminent attack. The ripping, groaning sounds resounded through the village, and, close by, Brenna heard a metallic clatter. She stepped back from the altar and pulled Samantha with her. The heavy labrys was vibrating violently, its twin blades beating a rapid-fire tattoo against the ancient rock.

"Sweet Gaia, lady." Kyla's voice was breathless. "The trees!"

Brenna spun, and the breath punched out of her lungs.

The inner ring of uniform trees that encircled the village was encased in a gray light that began to pulse and shimmer. Human figures were emerging through the gnarled bark of each tree. All women—heavily armed Amazon warriors, their bodies convulsing in apparent agony. The tortured moans rose from their fight to wrench themselves free of their dense wood prisons, leaving the trees unscathed. Seeming fully human, the warriors' faces were contorted in pain, their teeth bared in rage, and their eyes utterly insane.

"Jesstin, go." Shann's command came fast and clear. "The rest of you, hold here with me."

"Lady." Jess snapped her sword to point straight at Dana. "Dana, Brenna, you guard our queen's life." She paused on the brink of flight and faced Brenna, and her fingers moved in the subtle twirl that signaled an adonai's love. Then Jess whirled and was gone, the rising fog swallowing her with unsettling abruptness.

The spectral invaders were moving out of the trees now and closing in around the village. That they were Amazon was evident at first sight. The glyphs marking their faces were foreign to Brenna, but she recognized their distinctive weapons, and the cut of their armor was an old guild design.

A harrowing wail rose from the ghost warriors, an ancient battle cry corrupted by their unholy resurrection.

Their bloody screams were met at once by the rising tide of Tristaine's vocal fury, as the cries of Shann's Amazons rang their answering challenge. Brenna alone heard another sound—the monotonous, grieving undertone of an elderly woman's weeping.

Battle broke fast, and it was intense and vicious. The illumination provided by the fire and the eerily luminous fog allowed Brenna to discern shapes, and she followed Jess's streaking form with fierce concentration. Clashes broke out in rapid succession just outside the square, punishing hand-to-hand combat, and the undead Amazons matched Tristaine's warriors in both ferocity and skill.

Jess was everywhere, and for whole minutes at a time Brenna's fear for her surrendered to awe at the brutal grace of her dance. She fought with murderous precision, spinning from one opponent to the next, her sword cutting sizzling arcs. Brenna shuddered as Jess's blade plunged deep into the chest of one phantom enemy, and Samantha clenched her arm.

They watched the ghost-warrior spasm on Jess's sword, her arms splayed, and her eyes rolling whitely toward the night sky. Then the woman's body crumbled to dust, solid bulk melting to powder in less than a second. Jess staggered, thrown by the sudden lack of resistance at the end of her blade. She stepped back from the pile of sand at her boots, stunned, then turned and raced toward her next prey.

"Did you see—?" Samantha stammered.

"Shann!" Brenna peeled Sammy's fingers off her forearm.

"Yes, Brenna, these slaves of Botesh are mortal enough." Shann had both hands on the altar, as if to contain its power. Her calm voice helped steady Brenna through the rising chaos around them. "It seems our ghoul is content to hide behind her slaves. She'll not show her wretched face tonight."

"*Lady!*" Kyla's screamed warning came almost too late. The ghost-warrior roaring down on their right might have reached Shann, had Kyla not bolted past her and met the attack herself head-on.

The undead Amazon's dozen braids whipped around her head, and her dark skin gleamed with sweat in spite of the night's chill. She brandished two long daggers, and Brenna's heart almost stopped as Kyla flew at the warrior and tackled her around the waist. Her momentum slammed them both to the ground, but the alien woman recovered quickly, twisting free of Kyla and kneeling for a strike to her unprotected back.

There was a rush of motion at Brenna's side as Dana launched into the air, kicking off the altar for purchase and crashing bodily into the crouching Amazon. The two rolled free of Kyla, who scrambled to her feet, and Shann snatched her back out of harm's way.

Dana's features were fixed in a rictus as she twisted the leather thong of her sling around her enemy's neck. The maniacal light faded slowly from the struggling warrior's face, and in the dying moment before she shriveled to dust beneath Dana's hands, Brenna saw her eyes fill with a pathetic gratitude.

Kyla shook off Shann's concern and ran to kneel beside Dana. "Did she cut you?"

"No." Dana sat back on her heels, staring at her empty hands. Kyla touched her face.

The fighting was well contained outside the perimeter of the square. No other attacker came close to breaching that boundary. War cries blended with clashing steel and the screams of the wounded in the trees beyond them. A distant, spiraling whistle sounded.

"The first wounded are being brought in." Shann had to shout to be heard. "We'll be needed in the healing lodge. It looks like clear passage, sisters, but move with care."

"Shann, I want to join our healers in the field." Brenna's blood thrummed with an urgency to reach Jess. "I'll see you and Sam safely there."

"No, Brenna, you're with me. Our most gravely injured will be brought to the lodge."

"But, lady—"

"I said you're with me. Dana, hold." Shann caught Dana's arm as she started to lift the double-headed labrys from the altar. "That stays here, adanin. Dyan's blades will seal the lid of this vile creature's tomb." She swept off her white outer robe and wrapped it around a shivering Samantha. "We move, now!"

❖

Her nearly human ears heard the guardian's puling commands. Botesh fought to contain her ravenous fury.

It had been centuries. She could wait for one more dawn and the second rising of Thesmophoria's moon.

She would savor the juices of this woman's liver by its crimson light.

❖

The fog lifted in the fading hours of the night, as did the smoke from a dozen small fires set by thrown torches. The air was clean and clear again, and the sky was lush with stars only beginning to fade in the predawn light.

Brenna sat beside Samantha on a log bench several yards from the healing lodge. The fighting was largely over now. They still heard whistles signaling brief skirmishes at the far reaches of the mesa, but they were few and scattered. The night's battle was decided, and the sun would rise over a victorious Tristaine.

But at a horrendous price. Brenna rested her aching head in her hands and released a shaking sigh. There would be thirteen funeral pyres to build when this was over, if any in their clan lived to light them. And the final tally wasn't in. Dozens more were terribly wounded. She had never seen such carnage.

Jess had not returned yet.

Beside her, Sammy made a distressed gulping sound, and Brenna sat up and laid a sympathetic hand on her sister's leg. "You need to go again?"

"I might." Sammy swallowed convulsively.

"It's okay. Let fly. Just not on my boots, please."

"No. No." Samantha lifted a hand, her eyes closed. "I'm okay."

Brenna rubbed small circles on Samantha's back. "You sure?"

"Yeah. Just don't burp me."

"Can I get you anything?"

"A cigarette. God, Brenna. I'm sorry I made such a scene."

"Sammy, no. You were amazing. You saw stuff in there that would choke a buzzard, and you hung in there with us all night. You really helped."

"And I threw up," Samantha sighed. "And fainted. Then I woke up and threw up again."

"Sorry, the vomiting's genetic." Brenna checked Sammy's color. She was glad Shann had signaled to take her outside during this lull in casualties. Her own fear and fatigue were receding enough to allow real concern for her sister. Sammy had seen more than the gruesome butchery of combat tonight. The sterile and secular worldview of the City they had grown up in didn't allow for things like Amazon zombies. Brenna could only hope her own ability to absorb the bizarre without losing her sanity ran in the family too.

"Bree?" As if reading her mind, Samantha turned to her with a plaintive look. "Is it always so...*intense* around here?"

A bubble of laughter rose in Brenna's throat and died there.

Jess was walking toward them, weaving slowly through a stand of poplars across from the lodge.

Brenna shot to her feet. Even by fading moonlight, Jess was covered in an appalling amount of gore. But she was upright and mobile and gazing at Brenna with weary relief.

"Jesstin!" Vicar's shout was distant and ragged. "Bloody hell, Jess, stop!"

Jess lifted one blood-streaked arm toward Brenna and dropped to her knees.

Brenna's heart staggered in her chest. She ran hard, but she wasn't fast enough to catch Jess before she crumpled to the ground.

CHAPTER TEN

Bloody half-wit." Vicar paced the small cabin, her long step marred by a pronounced limp. "She wouldn't stop, lady. I saw the damned cretin take a dozen strikes. She was gushing like a geyser."

"Peace, Vicar."

Brenna appreciated Shann's stern tone. She already had too many faint-inducing images of Jess going down in her mind. She didn't need to add geysers to her nightmares. She helped Shann shake out a thick fur and spread it over their patient, who was still trembling like an aspen.

At least she had Jess home. Tristaine's healing lodge was crowded with wounded warriors, and the less critical cases were being taken to surrounding cabins. Brenna knew Jess would rest more easily here, in the oak bed fashioned by her own hands. And thanks to all the goddesses guiding Tristaine, her injuries didn't require their healers' constant care.

Jess was coming around again now, and Brenna sat on the bed and rested her hand against her bruised face. "Hey."

"Hey," Jess croaked. She started to sit up, and her eyes closed abruptly.

"Whoa, slow down, hotshot." Brenna eased Jess back down and smoothed the warm pelt across her chest. "You're home, Jess."

Jess squinted up at her, and her face softened. "Aye, that I am." She cleared her throat. "How long was I out?"

"It's just after dawn, Jesstin." Shann sat on the bed's

other side. "Can you stay with us a while? I know you're in pain. We can give you some tea to help you sleep soon. But I need a brief council before we let you rest."

"I'm able, lady." Jess drew as deep a breath as her aching sides would allow and pushed herself carefully higher against the cushions behind her. Brenna shifted and slid one arm behind Jess's neck to support her head. The solid warmth of Jess's body against her side was a blessed reassurance.

"Bleeding Hera, Jesstin." Vicar folded her arms and glared at her cousin. "Care to tell me what made you think you had to take out the entire demon horde single-handed?"

"Hush, Vicar, keep your voice down." Kyla was crouching beside Samantha, tucking her cloak around her sleeping form. Sammy was curled on the floor in front of the wide fieldstone fireplace, and Brenna doubted a shrieking banshee would wake her.

The small cabin Brenna shared with Jess was crowded with women they loved. Dana sat against one wall, watching Kyla with an open longing only exhaustion allowed her to reveal. Shann's elegant features had aged visibly during the endless night. She rose from the bed and went to Vicar.

"I promise, adanin, to castigate this rash warrior most harshly. But you've seen Jesstin safely home, Vicar. I want you to go get that ankle stitched."

"Wai Li can patch me later, Shann."

Shann shook her head. "I trust your adonai's skill with a needle, but go have her patch you now, please. I don't like your color."

"We don't like yer color, Vic," Jess echoed. She turned her head stiffly on Brenna's arm. "Go on, Stumpy. You're bleeding on my clean floor."

"I hear, lady." Vic scowled and jerked her chin toward Jess. "But if I see this shrimpy dolt out of her blankets before dusk, I'll flatten her again myself."

"I'm there," Dana offered.

"Vicar." Jess's voice gentled. "My thanks. You risked your neck to save mine a dozen times last night."

Vicar shrugged. "Always will." She nodded to Shann and stepped out of the cabin, letting in a brief flood of sunlight. Heavy curtains cast the small room in shadow, illuminated now only by the fire crackling in the hearth.

"Here, Shann. Lady." Dana unwound from her seat on the floor and carried a heavy chair to the side of the bed. "You look a bit wiped. Ma'am."

"Thank you, adanin." Shann accepted Dana's hand and, in spite of her weariness, lowered herself to the polished oak seat as gracefully as if it were a throne. She regarded Jess with clinical concern. "You're still shaking, Jesstin."

"I'm warming fast, lady." Jess's finger shifted beneath the fur and brushed over Brenna's breast, and Brenna smiled into her thick hair.

"But you've taken some punishing strikes." Shann slid the furs down carefully to reveal Jess's battered form, wrapped in several layers of bandages. Brenna closed her eyes, but then made herself match Shann's calm appraisal of her injuries. "Nothing mortal or even disabling, all thanks to our Mothers. But there are some vicious cuts here, and this one—" Her hand hovered over Jess's shoulder. "You've lost a great deal of blood, Jess. And this bruising runs deep." She laid gentle fingers on her lower left side.

"So I'll not rival Kimba's prowess tonight." Jess flexed her right arm. "I can still lift a sword."

"Not for long, dear one." Shann pulled the furs over Jess again. Brenna tried to catch her eye, but Shann avoided her gaze and addressed them all. "Our warriors fought like furies in this opening battle, adanin, and their valor carried us safe to morning. But our numbers are sadly depleted, and the Thesmophorian moon rises again tonight."

"Our enemies were Amazons." Kyla shook her head in bewildered sadness. "Not Tristaine, but part of the Nation. Our sisters, lady."

"They were the spirits of the warriors who lie in the graveyard west of the mesa. The tribe of the stone queen." Brenna shivered, remembering that dry, monotonous sobbing. "I heard her weeping as her clan attacked."

"Dear Goddess." Shann lowered her head. "I can't imagine enduring such grief."

A silence fell, broken only by the crackling of the fire. Kyla went to the hearth and lifted a pot of steaming water off the grate. Their cups held a variety of teas, and a light, pleasant blend of scents reached Brenna as Kyla filled them. Jess had stopped shivering and lay quietly beneath her stroking hand.

"The look on that warrior's face when she died," Dana said finally. She was staring at her hands in the firelight. "Like I was saving her life, not ending it. I think she welcomed death."

Shann nodded, warming her fingers around her mug. "As would any true Amazon compelled to murder her sisters, Dana. The warriors who fought Tristaine last night weren't *hers* any longer, our ancient stone queen. They still are not hers. Their souls belong to Botesh."

"It's why we beat them, Shann." Jess stirred beneath the furs. "The ghost-warriors were nearly our equal in skill, more than equal in numbers. But they fought with ferocity, not passion. They were forced into battle by a loathed demon. Tristaine willingly defended a queen we all cherish."

Shann's eyes shimmered, and she reached down and brushed a lock of Jess's hair off her forehead.

Kyla checked Samantha's sleep, then settled on the floor beside Dana. She lifted her hand into her lap and twined their fingers together.

"Shann." Brenna waited until she finally met her gaze.

"The souls of those warriors were imprisoned in the inner ring of trees that encircle the village. There's still the outer ring. It's much larger."

"Ah, lordy, she's right." Dana rested her head against the wall. "If that outer ring spits out Amazons tonight, there's going to be lots more of them."

"Enough to overwhelm our weakened forces." Shann said this calmly, as if she were not predicting the death of her clan. "That's why we must face Botesh herself at moonrise."

"Lady." Jess slid her scratched hand across the fur and covered Shann's. "It's time you told us your strategy."

Brenna saw Shann's gaze move to Samantha's sleeping face.

"Time and past time, Jesstin, yes. What there is of it." Shann sighed as though a weight were lifting from her shoulders. "You've all been patient with my silence, and I thank you for that. I can tell you this much."

Dana and Kyla both sat slightly straighter against the wall.

"I have heard and heeded the words of my adonai, sisters. I believe they reflect the will of our Goddess. I'm confident Her triad stands ready for Tristaine's defense. Their blended strength will rise tomorrow night when Botesh takes physical form on our mortal plane."

"But how will they fight Botesh, lady?" Jess asked. "What shape will this battle take?"

"Brenna." Shann smiled. "Tell me, why do I keep after you to record the life of our clan in your journal?"

"Because…" Brenna struggled for the right wording. "Because our history can provide a map for our granddaughters. The way Tristaine lives today can guide her descendants."

"Exactly." Shann nodded. "Amazon lives become legend, Jesstin. Our grandmothers have faced similar enemies in our history. Just as the tale of our talented singer warned us

of Botesh, Amazon myth carries clues to her downfall. Kyla...
how did Queen Lenea fight the demon-king who threatened
her tribe?"

"She conjured a naiad, who skewered the king with an
enchanted trident." Kyla blinked, then smiled grimly. "I'd love
to see Botesh skewered, lady, on any blade we can wield."

"No more than I, little sister." Shann's eyes glinted briefly
with a predatory light. "As for a concise strategy for our next
moonlight battle, adanin, I freely admit to having none. I'll
trust in our Mothers to guide us when the time comes."

"That's all the assurance we need, Shann." Brenna was
relieved to realize she still meant every word. This queen had
seen her clan whole through harrowing calamity before, and
Tristaine had risen from the dust at the end of the day.

"Thank you, Blades." Shann's tone warmed. "And now,
I order a period of much-needed rest, sisters. I'll find my bed
too, after I check Hakan's wound."

"Hakan?" Jess lifted herself on her elbows, ignoring
Brenna's restraining hand. "Is she badly hurt, lady?"

"She is, Jesstin." Shann's voice softened. "But our
sister has the strength of Artemis. She's one of many in my
prayers."

Shann stepped quietly to the hearth and looked down at
Samantha's sleeping face. Then she lifted her cloak from a peg
on the wall and wrapped it around her shoulders. She stopped
at the door and turned to Brenna.

"I wanted very much to shield you and Samantha from
this danger, Blades. But I'll not be able to keep either of you
out of it tonight. We'll need all your courage."

"You'll have it," Brenna promised. "But Shann, what
will we—"

"Peace, little sister. You'll know in time." Shann's fingers
formed a gentle, twirling shape in the air, a benediction, and
then she was gone.

Brenna rested her cheek in Jess's hair and stared at the fire. Samantha was snoring softly, a mild, soporific buzzing Brenna had teased her about throughout their childhood.

Dana nudged Kyla and patted her thigh, and Kyla stretched out and rested her head in her lap. Dana saw Brenna watching them and smiled at her with wistful sweetness, her fingers trailing through Kyla's hair.

Jess let out a sharp breath and tightened suddenly, her eyes closing.

"Here, honey." Brenna braced Jess's head and held a cup to her lips. "Drink the rest of this. It'll help you sleep."

Jess swallowed the tea without protest, which told Brenna much about the pain of her injuries. She set the empty cup aside and stroked her hair, willing her to relax.

"Do we nurture a new seer, Bren?"

"Hm?" Brenna followed Jess's gaze to Samantha, sound asleep near the hearth. She remembered the confusion in her sister's eyes when she asked about *j'heika.* "Oh, lord. I'd forgotten, Jess."

"Did your Sammy show any gift for prophecy growing up, lass?"

"Well, we weren't exactly tested for such things, but no. Neither did I, for that matter."

"Your first visions came when you joined Tristaine?"

"My first visions came when I met you." Brenna kissed the top of Jess's head. "I wonder if this seer thing tends to run in families."

"A talent for queasiness seems to." Jess grinned, and her eyes drifted closed.

"You have to rest, love."

"Tell me the names first, Bren."

"Ah, Jesstin. It can wait. Please, you really need to—"

"I need to hear the names."

So Brenna drew Jess closer, held her with great care, and

began the terrible litany.

"We lost Ayla," she whispered. "And Remy, and Elodia. Raven fell. Perry is gone, and Trenare, and Danai, and Cyrene..."

Jess's tears fell silently and blended with Brenna's. Only when the last fallen warrior was named did they surrender to sleep.

CHAPTER ELEVEN

Pounding on the cabin door woke Brenna seemingly seconds later. Jess jerked out of sleep, then gasped and clutched the furs in a white-knuckled grip. Brenna cursed softly and steadied her, trying to clear the cobwebs from her mind.

Dana trotted to the door, scrubbing one hand over her face. She snatched it open, and Brenna was alarmed when no flood of sunlight filled the cabin. Surely it couldn't be much past noon. Kyla and Samantha were both sitting up, looking as groggy and disoriented as she felt.

"Back up, weed." Sarah tapped her walking stick irritably at Dana's legs as she entered, then peered into the cabin's dark interior with a scowl. "Jesstin? You in here?"

"I'm here, grandmother." Jess sat up slowly, waving off Brenna's hand. "Is there—"

"Fog's falling. Moon's rising. Shanendra calls you all to the square." Sarah turned and waved her stick at Dana again to get her out of the way.

"Wait, hold up—ow." Dana hopped back. "Sarah, why's it so dang dark out?"

"Do I look like an oracle?" Sarah growled. "All I know is the sun took it in its mind to set half a day early. I've got three more messages to deliver. Fog's falling, moon's rising, and Shanendra calls you all to the square. Any more impertinent questions?"

"None." Dana looked out the cabin door, shaking her head before closing it after Sarah.

"Easy, Jess." Brenna darted around the bed and took Jess's arm as she pulled herself upright. Jess wavered for a moment, grimacing, then seemed to find her center. She straightened, holding her left side.

"My gear, Bren?"

"Jesstin, listen to sense." Brenna gripped her wrist. "You can hardly stand, much less fight. You can't possibly—"

"My place is at our queen's side, lass." Jess brushed one finger down the side of Brenna's face. "Help me dress, and I'll thank you for it. But I fight tonight, with or without your help."

Brenna held Jess's rough palm to her cheek and tried to quell the burning in her stomach. "If you fight, I'll have your back, Jess. My place is with you."

Jess smiled, then bent her head and kissed her, a languid, sweet exploration of lips and tongue, a fleeting moment of peace before chaos fell.

❖

At first it seemed to Brenna a nightmare replay of the previous evening, running beside Jess through the curdled fog, Amazons streaming in all directions, urgent whistles calling summons to battle. But this night's race held a macabre new element that cast a gruesome glow over Tristaine's mesa. The Thesmophorian moon cresting the horizon was a deep bloodred.

Jess inserted two fingers in her mouth and sent out an ear-piercing trilogy of notes, and Brenna heard it answered from three different sectors seconds later. If Botesh hoped to catch Shann's women flat-footed by somehow hastening the night, her plan was failing. Even depleted, Tristaine's warriors were highly trained and formidable fighters, and there was no panic in their preparations.

Every woman and child in Tristaine might become a warrior before the night was through, Brenna thought. She and Kyla carried escrima sticks, thin rods made of hard rock maple, nearly two feet long. Wielding them required skill, and Brenna had become adept in their use over the past summer. Even Samantha was armed with a short, stout club for self-defense should the fighting close in. She ran with them silently, almost as pale as Jess.

Jess was moving well, her long stride relaxed and even. She still held her left side, but her breathing came easily, and Brenna marveled again at the healing capacity of Amazon stock.

The silence was getting to her. Except for the light pattering of their feet and the occasional whistled signal, the premature night was quiet as a graveyard. Brenna saw the altar in the distance, long before they entered the square. It seemed to glow with its own malevolence, in resonant harmony with the crimson moon.

If the bloody moonlight embraced the altar as kin, it outlined Tristaine's queen in a more benevolent silhouette. The fog swirled in restless coils around Shann's robes, but she ignored its clammy touch, every line of her body resolute.

As Shann had commanded, the six women were alone in the village square. Jess unleashed another series of whistles as they gathered in its center, and a volley of distant replies came quickly.

"We're in place, Shann." Jess straightened and dropped her hand from her side. "The first wave monitors the outer ring. The second waits a hundred yards farther in."

"And we're the third wave, if need be." Shann's smile was grim. "Pity Botesh if she does regain her humanity tonight. Flesh gives more easily than spirit to Tristaine steel."

Shann's clear voice echoed in the fog-shrouded square, and Brenna felt a thrill of dark anticipation. She had seen this side of Shann before, on the brink of an earlier battle, when Tristaine was threatened by Caster. She was healer, teacher, and much more, but tonight, Shann was once again a blood-tested queen of warrior women, and any victory Botesh might eke out would be dearly won.

"Hear me, adanin." Shann walked before them, meeting the eyes of each woman as she passed. "Our sisters cry out from their graves for justice. Tonight we end the reign of a traitorous queen whose hands are drenched in centuries of Amazon blood."

A low tapping sound reached Brenna, and she was afraid her trip-hammering heart was audible in the silence of the square. But then she recognized the source of the metallic clatter. Dyan's labrys still lay on the altar's surface, and its blades were vibrating again against the black rock. The heavy weapon quivered with power, as if holding back a furious force determined to break free.

Shann reacted at once, her robes swirling as she went to the altar. A cry formed and died in Brenna's throat as Shann gripped the labrys in both hands and lifted it, stilling its tremors.

"Lady, listen!" Jess drew her sword from its scabbard, and Dana mirrored her action. Kyla stepped protectively closer to Samantha, the escrima wands braced and ready in her hands. Sammy looked around wildly, her club hovering over her shoulder like a baseball bat.

Brenna heard it then, and her heartbeat ratcheted higher. That terrible low moaning, repellant at a visceral level. The outer ring of trees that encircled Tristaine was too far distant to see from the square, but Brenna didn't need her eyes. The far-off, guttural groaning meant the bark of each tree had begun to shimmer with that ghastly gray light. It was the first sign of the emergence of the ghost-warriors.

Jess was poised and ready for flight. "Shann, send me on."

"Not tonight, Jesstin. We'll need your protection here." Shann carried the labrys around the altar and walked back to them. "Keep them off us, Jess, as long as you possibly can."

"Lady—"

"And have more faith in your warrior-sisters, Jesstin. Remember, our enemies are forced into battle by a loathed demon." Shann stopped in front of Brenna and held the labrys out to her. "Tristaine's warriors fight willingly to defend a queen we all cherish."

Brenna looked at her, then at the labrys, then at Shann again. "Oh, no. No, you don't. You're not giving me that. Don't you pull this queen stuff on me now, Shanendra. I'm entirely serious."

"Tristaine's sacred blades are too heavy for me to carry alone tonight, little sister." Shann's eyes were compassionate. "And they are your birthright. You're simply going to have to suck it up."

Shann dropped the labrys, and Brenna's hands shot out to catch it before it touched the ground. She tried to mumble further protest, but Shann turned abruptly to the altar.

"Botesh!" Shann's voice was sharp as a whiplash, cutting through the distant moaning. "Blight on the Nation, I invoke you!"

"She's *invoking* her?" Dana was turning to keep the square in view, her sword held ready. "What the hell do we do if she *answers*?"

"She'll answer. She has to." Brenna hefted the labrys in her hands, glaring holes in Shann's back. "Undead or not, Botesh is Amazon. She can't ignore the direct command of another Amazon queen. A *real* queen!" she yelled to Shann.

The wretched groaning was growing louder. Brenna's

inner eye focused on the largest ring of trees again and the twisted shapes beginning to emerge from the gnarled trunks.

"I compel you, demon, rise!" Shann cried.

The top of the altar cracked with a thunderous concussion so jarring Samantha dropped her club and clapped her hands to her ears. A jagged line streaked down the center of the altar's stone surface, and from its depths Botesh rose.

At first the ghost-queen was more sound than anything visible. Botesh manifested as an innocuous tendril of smoke weaving above the altar, ephemeral, saturated with red moonlight. But the sounds that rose with the fiend's spirit revealed her nature more vividly than a hideous appearance could. Brenna heard the terrified screams of hundreds of women issuing from the cracked altar, and she nearly dropped the labrys in shock. These heartrending cries were a sound Botesh carried with her as a gangrenous wound carried a stench.

Brenna heard whistles from the outer reaches of the mesa, signaling imminent attack.

"Who should I thank for allowing me to witness your bloody deaths?"

Brenna saw Jess raise her sword as the sibilant voice whispered from the stream of smoke, and she was grateful that at least they all heard it. The opening remarks of their unwelcome guest didn't lend much hope for diplomacy, but that had never really been an option. Tristaine didn't bargain with murderers forever banished from Gaia's light.

"Don't count your scalps too soon, putrescent queen." Shann stood almost casually, with her hands clasped behind her. Her words were etched in acid, but a small smile played over her lips. "You have no idea who you're dealing with."

"Oh, I'll savor your screams, old woman." Something horribly like laughter shuddered through the smoke. "Your death throes will be like a thousand tongues on my sex."

War cries, both mortal and inhuman, broke out all over the mesa, and Brenna's blood chilled. The fighting was on in earnest.

"The slaughter begins." The red smoke wavered for an instant into a recognizably female form, then dissolved again. "You'll be butchered by the finest Amazon army that ever marched, doomed hag. I have collected my warriors from all over the world, and they are unstoppable."

"Those same warriors beg for a death they prefer to serving you, corruption."

The harrowing screams that flowed from Botesh's presence flared, as if to answer Shann's claim. The fear in those cries shook Brenna badly and made it difficult to think.

"I'll bathe in the blood of you and your Kores by dawn, Shanendra. And I'll take a small sample now."

"Shann!"

Brenna heard Jess's warning cry, but Botesh struck before any of them could act. A dart of smoke shot from the undulating stream and struck Shann full in the chest. She flew off her feet and landed hard, breaking Brenna's paralysis. Brenna ran to the fallen queen, just as Jess bolted past them.

Jess's sword carved through the column of smoke with savage power but had no effect on the nebulous spirit. Jess backed up a step and assumed a defensive stance between Shann and the demon who hovered above the altar.

"Is it bad, Bree?" Samantha dropped to her knees at Shann's other side and helped Brenna raise her to a sitting position. Her eyes were half-open but unfocused.

"Shann, you've had the breath knocked out of you." Brenna's hands were gentle as she opened the top of Shann's robe. She spoke as if the still woman could hear her. "It's a surface wound, lady. There's no vital damage."

The adrenaline pumping through Brenna's veins subsided enough to allow a moment of relief. Botesh's weapon had scored three deep scratches across the top of Shann's left breast, an inch from her heart. They bled sluggishly, but hadn't penetrated deeply enough to threaten her life. She was regaining her senses now, and Brenna saw her breathing ease into a pattern designed to both calm and strengthen the heart.

"Your blood christens the dawn of my new reign, Shanendra." The column of smoke flexed, and drops of red fell from it to spatter on the cracked surface of the altar below. Steam rose where the blood splashed on stone. "Your warriors have begun to die again. I welcome them to the ranks of my screaming disciples. They will make my army truly invincible."

"Jesstin!" Dana paused as a strident whistle split the night, rising above the bloodcurdling war cries in the forest. "Our first line is falling back!"

The fighting was getting closer, the ghost-warriors closing in on the square. Brenna could hear the clash of steel on steel now, and the terrible screams of horses.

"Brenna." Shann closed her eyes for a long moment, and when they opened they were clear and shining. She studied Brenna's face and Samantha's. "I wanted to spare you both this trial, dear ones. But it's time for you to remember."

Brenna felt a chill course through her. "Okay. Remember what?"

"Joanna." Shann slid one hand beneath Samantha's hair to cup her neck. "Rebecca." Her other hand warmed Brenna's neck. "It's time for you to remember me."

Sammy looked as mystified as Brenna felt.

"This butcher called you my Kores." Shann shot a contemptuous glance toward the altar. "Who is Kore, Brenna?"

"Kore is another name for Persephone." Brenna answered automatically. "Demeter's daughter…"

She felt the light warmth of Shann's hand cradling her

neck, and her throat constricted. Some deep part of her, long since scarred over, remembered this touch in a new way. Her cellular memory summoned the feel of this woman's hand holding her much smaller one and the image of Shann's younger face, smiling above her. She had filled her sky once.

Brenna looked at Sammy and saw the same blend of confusion and recognition dawning on her face.

Shann's hand slid from Brenna's neck to cup her face. "You were both taken from me soon after Joanna's birth. It's that loss that drove me to Tristaine, Brenna."

Dana let out a piercing whistle. "Jess, right flank!"

One of Botesh's undead warriors had broken through the trees and was racing for the square. She was an enormous Amazon, dressed in an alien tangle of furs and leather, and outlined in a sick green light. Spittle flew from her clenched teeth as she raised her battle axe, and Brenna could see she was targeting directly on Shann.

"Back off, bruja!" Jess clasped the hilt of her sword in both hands and was at full speed within three strides. She charged directly into the screaming warrior's path and engaged her in a sparking strike of steel.

"Brenna. Look at me." Shann gripped her chin in strong fingers, forcing Brenna's attention away from Jess. "There's no time. Pick up the labrys."

"Brenna!" Samantha sounded scared. She pointed to the other end of the square, where two more ghost-warriors emerged from the trees. Dana and Kyla were off like a shot to head them off.

"The labrys, Brenna!" Shann commanded.

Brenna looked around, dazed, and saw Dyan's ancient weapon on the ground a few feet away. She had dropped it there in her haste to get to Shann. She stretched out and grabbed it and pulled it into her lap.

"Samantha. Your hand, please." Shann positioned

Sammy's fingers on the head of the two-bladed axe. "Brenna, keep your grip on the hilt of our deliverer."

Brenna was shaking hard. Her heart and soul were with Jess, twenty yards away, alone and battling a growing weakness. The undead warrior she fought was still striving with ghoulish determination to reach Shann. But the compelling urgency in Shann's voice kept Brenna focused on the leather-wrapped hilt, her fingers curling around it with desperate strength.

Shann's hand hovered over the midsection of the labrys, then settled around it and held on. Brenna felt an instant pulse of power that was nearly painful, an electric current shooting through her blood. Kneeling across from her, Samantha flinched, too, but kept her hand on the cold blade.

Music. As naturally as screams accompanied Botesh, a strange, thrumming harmony flowed from the labrys, once galvanized by the joining of the Crone, the Mother, and the Maiden. A gold light seeped from it, bathing them in a soft glow.

"Only an Amazon queen, an equally powerful light matched to her darkness, can vanquish this evil." Brenna heard Dyan's voice.

The ethereal light filling the labrys brightened, glowing red through the three hands that touched it. Brenna looked at Shann's face and into the eyes of the Crone. Superimposed over Shann's features was the weathered visage of an old woman, patience and wisdom shining in her gaze.

Brenna turned to Samantha and saw her pale and worried expression strengthened by the mature, protective countenance of the Mother. Brenna touched her own face and knew the fresh innocence of the Maiden looked out at the world through her eyes.

The music of the labrys grew rich and full, empowered by the joining of these three aspects of the Goddess.

Brenna heard another woman speak, her tone deep and

resonant. *"When Tristaine is in deepest tribulation, She will be led by three generations of blood-bonded queens."*

And yet another Woman spoke in Brenna's mind, and hers alone. Not Dyan or Shann or Jess or any other earthly advisor, but the Voice that always offered this challenge.

J'heika, rise.

Brenna decided to take Her literally. She rose in one smooth movement, carrying the glowing labrys with her. In this world, it had always been a rugged axe made of wood and steel. Now it was much more, a deadly weapon charged with the blended energies of three faces of the Goddess, three Amazons of royal blood.

Brenna stalked toward the altar, growing more furious with every heartbeat. The square was filling with battling warriors now, both Botesh's damned and Tristaine's fighters, and the noise was hideous. But Brenna's ear was tuned to the strange aria of the labrys, and she faced Botesh without flinching.

The broad flat stone that served as the altar's surface had canted to one side when the vile essence of the malignant spirit burst from its depths. The glyphs etched into the rock glittered in the red moonlight, and one in particular gleamed brightest.

The drops of Shann's blood had carved a new sigil on the craggy plate. Seven drops, in a configuration at once so beloved and familiar to Brenna, and so shocking in this profane context, it almost brought her to her knees. It was the Seven Sisters, Tristaine's star clan—and Botesh's diabolical claim of ownership.

"Greetings, young queen," the sibilant voice purred above her. "Your nubile loveliness is wasted among these barbarians. I will make you my personal bed slave when I regain form. You will watch my own hand squeeze the life from this hag's frail neck."

"You will shut up," Brenna said calmly. "And you will

keep your putrid claws off my *mother, bitch!*"

The labrys swung up, its music flaring. Then Brenna brought it down with immense power on the altar's cracked surface.

The stone block imploded with a titanic shock. Shards of black rock ricocheted crazily, and the scarlet cloud that was Botesh spasmed higher into the air.

In the next second, in the void created when the altar crumbled, an Amazon Warrior stood.

She was easily ten feet tall, entirely solid and definitely real. Gleaming ebony skin, powerfully muscled, shielded by armor, a broadsword sheathed on her back. The woman regarded Brenna silently.

Brenna took a step back, still clenching the labrys in her frozen hands. If this behemoth belonged to Botesh…and then Shann appeared beside her and spoke to the warrior.

"Well met, Kimba. Welcome home."

Brenna's jaw dropped, and all she could do for a moment was mouth the name and stare.

Kimba's glittering eyes moved to Samantha, who stepped numbly up between Shann and Brenna.

Tristaine's first and greatest warrior took a step forward and dropped to one knee before the Crone, the Mother, and the Maiden. Her dark head, curtained with tight black braids bound with chips of ivory and bone, dipped in respect.

Then Kimba rose, unsheathed her sword, and let loose a war cry that blew Brenna's hair back like a fierce wind. Obsidian eyes flashed with blood lust, and powerful legs propelled the huge warrior fast into the square and the thick of the fighting.

"Shann!"

Brenna spun as a frantic voice called from the edge of the square. The roiling fog obscured detail, but she could see a distant figure waving her arms.

"Lady, we have injured!"

"I'll come, adanin!" Shann turned to Brenna and clasped her shoulders.

"I'll see to our most seriously wounded, Brenna, and return as soon as I can. Look after your sister." Brenna nodded dumbly, dazed all over again by the realization that this woman's blood coursed through her veins.

"Soon we'll have a nice talk." Shann smiled, gave Brenna a swift kiss on the forehead, and moved quickly toward the edge of the square.

"Uh, Bree? Brenna?" Samantha plucked her sleeve. She was staring at the burned patch of ground that marked the altar's outline. There was a great roiling in the darkness of that hole; then, even as Brenna watched, another spectral Amazon fighter emerged from its depths. A third followed close behind, leading what became a steady stream of Tristaine's lost warriors.

"It's all right, Sammy." Brenna lifted an arm around Samantha's trembling shoulders. "They're ours."

She knew there would be time to teach Sammy all their names later, when the survivors of this battle recounted its marvels before storyfires. Brenna recognized most of these warriors by the vivid descriptions that were part of Amazon folklore. These were fighters out of Tristaine history and legend.

Ikarias, trained by Kimba herself, who liberated her tribe from its patriarchal oppressors. Trenare, who appeared with her adanin Barkida and Klymene, a trio of deadly archers who rescued a queen held captive in the City. Cerdryn, who perfected the clan's unique brand of hand-to-hand fighting.

More warriors came surging out of the earth, their armor and gear evolving from primitive to more recent cuts. Brenna counted fifty at least, hypnotized by the brutally armed parade.

She became aware of a pervasive buzzing sound and realized it was coming from the fluttering cloud that was Botesh, still hovering above the destroyed altar. The insectile hiss had replaced any power of speech she commanded.

And the quality of the spirit-women's screams that rose with Botesh was changing. Their fear was becoming fury. Despairing cries of terror were growing stronger, turning into a full-throated roar for justice.

"What's happening, Bree?" Samantha was trying for composure, but there was a definite quaver in her voice.

"We've called in our third wave." Brenna craned to see Jess through the fog and dust kicked up by the several skirmishes that had broken out in the square. She couldn't find her, and her heart pounded against her ribs in slow, leaden thuds.

"Is that her?"

"Who, Sam?"

"*Her!*"

Dyan was striding toward them, towering and magnificent. She stood with her massive fists on her hips, her dark eyes on Brenna. She stretched out one hand. "I'm here for what's mine, lass."

The labrys quivered on the ground by Brenna's foot, then shot aloft and sailed to Dyan's waiting grip. She fingered a chip in one gleaming blade, and her lip curled in outrage. "I'm not believin' ye chipped my axe!"

"I'm not believing you pushed me off a *cliff*," Brenna retorted.

Dyan grinned, a stunning flash of white teeth. "See to my lady's protection, Brenna."

"Dyan, please. See to mine."

"Jesstin." Dyan spoke the name with great affection, and then she was gone.

The square was bedlam, with deadly clashes every few

yards, leaving writhing bodies in their wake. More and more of those corpses crumbled to dust under Tristaine's growing power.

Tears rose in Brenna's eyes as other familiar faces began to emerge from the black altar's grave.

Myrine, Jess's close friend, who had stayed behind to ensure Caster's death when the flood drowned their valley last year. Theryn, who redeemed her honor by dying beside Myrine in Tristaine's defense.

And Camryn, streaking back into the world, pure Amazon pride incarnate, flush with the ancient honor of raising arms to protect her queen. Sirius, restored and whole. And then Ayla, Remy, and others lost to Tristaine only last night.

Breathless, Brenna scanned the trees where she'd last seen Jess. For a few terrifying minutes, she couldn't find her. The red moonlight ignited the boiling fog around her knees into a scarlet soup, and the trees were a chaos of fighting women.

The tide was turning quickly for Tristaine. Even as her living warriors flagged, her army of immortals overwhelmed Botesh's dispirited forces. Again and again, Brenna saw that poignant gratitude on the faces of the dying ghost-warriors.

Across the square, Kimba took out two undead Amazons with one harrowing swing of her sword. Closer by, Dana and Kyla, apparently unhurt, fought side by side with Camryn against a faltering trio of opponents.

The harsh snap of static buzzed loudly in Brenna's ears, a raw, ugly sound. She turned back to the shattered altar and the almost-forgotten specter that still hovered above it. The twisting tendril of smoke that was Botesh flickered like a sinister shroud in a fierce gale. She was the source of the hissing crackle that filled Brenna's mind, the same cacophony that provided the dissonant background of her first vision.

Even as Brenna watched, the mist above the altar drifted and diffused, then began to form again. A vaguely feminine figure materialized, suffused with a murky scarlet light. In her physical incarnation, Botesh's body held womanly contours and all the grace and allure of a bristling tarantula.

"Samantha!" Brenna was unable to take her eyes from the burgeoning shape of the Amazon sorceress. Samantha's hand clasped hers, and Brenna held on tight.

The face of Botesh was forming now. Brenna felt Samantha sag beside her as she absorbed one horror too many, and she slid a firm arm around her waist. The hatred blazing from Botesh's features felt like the dry skittering of that tarantula across a sweat-soaked back.

The powerful figure of Botesh rose higher in the air. She appeared only marginally human. The skin of the undead queen was armored with small interconnected scales, and her jaws widened to expose multiple rows of wickedly sharp fangs. Brenna learned there were worse things than the horror of Botesh's eyes—like the guttural, rasping fury of her reborn voice.

"Harlot queen!" Botesh lifted a broadsword as long as Brenna was tall and swung it around her head.

Brenna realized the half-demon was not targeting her and Samantha. She whirled and saw her intended victim. Shann was running, but she had not yet reached the center of the village square. She was nowhere near any cover, and none of Tristaine's warriors were close enough to defend her. Brenna screamed Shann's name in warning, but her voice was drowned out by the ear-splitting shriek Botesh released as she attacked.

Shann saw the raving queen streaking toward her, and she stood still, her body braced and centered.

Samantha gasped and pulled hard on Brenna's shoulder, forcing her down. Brenna looked up just in time to see two other figures in full flight above them.

Dyan's fist was snarled in the torn leather of Jess's

collar, hauling her bodily through space with her. In midair, they thudded in tandem against the very solid back of their adversary, and Botesh dropped under their joined fury like a raving beast brought down by dogs.

The impact of their landing scattered the rancid fog still carpeting the village square. Botesh's newly human form held the same size and power Dyan commanded in this world, and she jumped immediately to her feet.

Dyan and Jess fought together like the two lifelong friends and sisters in arms they were, each mirroring the other's deadly thrusts. The beauty of their brutal dance all but hypnotized Brenna, but they fought a formidable enemy.

Botesh injected centuries of repressed wrath into every wide swing of her sword, and the hissing static emanating from her scarlet skin made it difficult to focus. She seemed tireless, spinning to parry every blow from Jess's sword and Dyan's double-headed axe.

Part of Brenna watched Shann as she circled the fierce battle toward her and Samantha, her eyes riveted on Dyan. Brenna grabbed Shann's hand as she reached them and pulled her close, encircling her with one arm and Samantha with the other.

J'heika, rise.

Samantha didn't seem to hear the challenge this time, but it rang clearly in Brenna's mind. *"I'll trust in our Mothers to guide us when the time comes,"* Shann's silent voice repeated, and that guidance was there. Brenna knew immediately what she had to do.

"Dyan!" Brenna roared, with a force that stripped her throat raw, and she held out one hand. "Tristaine's blade!"

Dyan spun at the command and faced Brenna, and she, too, obeyed immediately. Her labrys left her grip and sailed through the air in a gentle arc, and its hilt smacked into Brenna's open palm.

Brenna balanced the axe in both hands and looked at Shann. Shann smiled down at Brenna with pure pride and touched the hilt. At Brenna's nod, Samantha rested her fingers on one of the labrys's gleaming blades.

Brenna clenched her jaw as the shock of power coursed through her body again, reuniting her with her mother on one side and her sister on the other. The labrys, regenerated by the combined energies of the Crone, Mother, and Maiden, sparked again with divine light.

"Jesstin!" Brenna bellowed.

Jess, fighting solo now, was hard-pressed to fend off Botesh's ruthless advance. She finally twisted free and dodged past her opponent, then whirled to see Brenna.

Brenna took the labrys in both hands and hurled it to Jess, praying fervently to her Mothers or Grandmothers or anyone else who could possibly guide her often errant aim.

Which was perfect. Jess dropped her sword, surged up, and snatched the glowing labrys out of the air, spinning before her boots hit the earth. She braced herself and snarled into Botesh's frothing face.

"Your granddaughters will mock your grave, Amazon."

It was the worst fate imaginable in their Nation.

Jess swung the shining labrys with all the power she had, and one curved blade punched deeply into Botesh's chest.

The effect was immediate and gruesome in the extreme. Botesh exploded in a torrent of foul-smelling blood, so copious it seemed her human form held no viscera, no bones, just an appalling flood of crimson. Jess and Dyan were both liberally spattered, and they staggered back.

The hideous static filling the square went silent, so abruptly the sudden lack of chaos was disorienting in itself.

Brenna drew a series of quick, deep breaths, fighting off a surge of light-headedness. She felt Shann leave her side, and she turned to Samantha.

"Sammy, I want you to sit down."

"Okay." Samantha folded her legs and plunked down immediately. Brenna knew she had seen enough. Her nerves had to be flash-fried.

She patted her sister's head, then ran past her. The square was filling again with Tristaine's warriors, cheering raggedly. What was left of Botesh's Amazon army had disintegrated en masse with her last sulfuric breath. Brenna sighted Jess and arrowed straight for her. She had dropped to the ground in exhaustion, but was already sitting up when Brenna fell to her knees beside her.

"Jesstin—"

"Bent," Jess gasped. "Not broken." She lifted a hand to forestall any other questions until she could catch her breath. Brenna braced her until she was reasonably sure she could stay upright.

"Sit still." Brenna whipped off her linen sash and folded it, then pressed it against the deep, seeping cut across Jess's shoulder. "You wrecked all my good stitchery, ace."

"Doesn't hurt."

"Macha crap, this doesn't hurt." She checked her pulse, then pulled the torn and bloody topshirt aside to examine her ribs.

"I'm just spent, Bren." Jess still struggled to draw an even breath.

Brenna ripped a strip of fabric from her topshirt and bound Jess's lower leg. "I remember ordering you not to lose any more blood."

"The night's ending, Brenna."

Jess was right. The trees were taking on that whispered illumination that came before the first hint of dawn. The red moon was less florid now, its malignant light weaker. The false night Botesh had summoned was giving way to first light.

"Come here. Let's get you warm." Brenna shifted

behind Jess so she could lean back into her arms. The move was strategic. Jess really did need her body heat. Both of them needed the physical contact. But Brenna also wanted a private moment to let her feelings play across her face, without worrying Jess. They were both shaking, Jess obviously with cold and shock, and Brenna with profound relief.

The extinction of the villainous queen had freed the souls of the warriors she had imprisoned in Tristaine's trees. Brenna held Jess and watched an amazing light show unfold. Streams of individual glowing sparks were ascending into the night sky in two separate directions. One stream arced toward the north and the star system those Amazons called home.

"Those are the spirits of the stone queen's clan." Brenna pointed to the other river of sparks, spinning eastward toward their own constellation. "And those are the souls of Botesh's tribe. It looks like Tristaine freed three clans tonight."

"How do you know all that?" Jess squinted at the same sparks. "I'm seeing pretty little lights."

"You want me to be a seer? Hush and let me see."

"Yes'm."

Tristaine's own immortal warriors were leaving now, returning home. They were a stream of brilliant silver lights, spiraling slowly up toward the Seven Sisters, still faintly visible overhead. There were several figures—Tristaine's most recent fallen—who lingered for a last farewell. In the distance, Brenna saw Camryn's glowing form standing close to Kyla.

Nearby, Dyan and Shann spoke quietly, inches apart. Dyan's larger figure loomed over Shann, but the exquisite tenderness between them was unmistakable. Brenna could see Shann's eyes, and they glowed with a profound joy. The words exchanged by these adonai were for their ears alone.

Finally, Dyan turned and walked toward Brenna and Jess. She put her hands on her hips and grinned down at them with fond pride. "I've come to give ye what's yours, Jesstin."

Jess had dropped the black labrys after it pierced Botesh's gory heart. Dyan gestured, and the two-headed axe rose from the ground and drifted lazily to Jess's open hands. Her fingers closed around the hilt, and Brenna felt tears rising in her eyes.

"You and I are champions of Amazon queens, adanin." Dyan nodded toward Brenna. "Serve your lady well."

"With my life, teacher." Jess answered with a title considered a high honorific in Tristaine.

Dyan sketched a blessing in the air and was gone.

Jess relaxed in Brenna's arms like a tired child, and she cradled her like one. That Jess would allow such a public display of weakness told Brenna all she needed to know about her exhaustion. She had to get her to the healing lodge soon, and there would be urgent need for her own skills there.

But for now, in this brief lull between battle and rebirth, Brenna and Jess held each other and watched the sun rise.

CHAPTER TWELVE

Six days later

Brenna clenched her teeth against the vicious sting and counted backward from ten.

"The needle does smart a bit," Jess had said. Jess had said *lots* of things since Brenna met her. She ruled supreme in the abyss-is-ditch, mountains-are-hills, Amazon art of understatement.

Between the fiery jabs, Brenna released a deep breath and searched for distraction, something to focus on other than the burning at the base of her throat. She closed her eyes and thought of her father. Shann's low voice filled her mind again, telling her two daughters the story of her first love.

"His name was David, and he was a good man." The fire-light played over Shann's fine features. Brenna and Samantha sat on cushioned chairs in her private cabin, warmed by the crackling fire in the hearth. Jess stood close by, listening, her arms folded. She had healed well in the days since the final battle.

"David and I fought in the same cell of the Resistance," Shann continued, "before the City Government hunted down and destroyed its leaders. We had two daughters before David was murdered and I was imprisoned. I was told my children died in the same explosion that killed my husband. They released me after four years in Prison, and I was exiled from the City."

Shann fell silent, gazing at her hands folded in her lap.

"And how did you find Tristaine?" Brenna asked gently. She didn't want to interrupt the flow of this sad history.

"Tristaine found me." Shann looked up and smiled at them. "Dyan and several of our sisters came across my sorry self, lying unconscious in a ravine high in the foothills. I'd been wandering for days, perhaps weeks. There were rumors of settlements in the mountains, and I had some vague notion of finding one. I'd passed out from hunger, and it's a simple miracle Dyan's patrol discovered me. The first of many miracles."

Shann lifted a kettle from a grate near the hearth and refilled their mugs with steaming cider. "My Dyan was a miracle in herself. I never dreamed I'd find love again. Certainly not that love, that powerful, bone-deep sense of rightness and belonging I felt in Dyan's arms. So my Mothers delivered me to my destiny with this clan, this family of Amazons, and the lifemate They always intended for me. And I never went back."

Shann put down the kettle, rose from her chair, and went to the window. "I believed what the City told me, and I never went back for my daughters. I've suspected our bond almost as long as I've known you, Brenna. I was too much of a coward to tell you earlier."

Brenna cleared her throat. "Why a coward?"

"I didn't want to admit to either of us that I'm a mother who abandoned her children."

"Lady," Jess said quietly, "you didn't know."

"I didn't question." Shann raked her fingers slowly through her hair. "I had better reason than most to suspect the City's duplicity, Jesstin, yet I accepted their death sentences as blind fact."

"When I heard your voice emerge from the stone queen, Shann," Brenna said, "you told me you were sorry."

"I have no conscious memory of those words, dear one, but I can validate the message. My heart has been saying something very like that to you, and your sister, for twenty years."

"And when I gave you Dyan's instructions for fighting Botesh?" Brenna asked. *"I saw your face, Shann. You looked scared."*

"Terrified," Shann confirmed. *"Just when I'd discovered you both, when I finally had you and Samantha back, safe and whole—Dyan tells me I must expose my daughters to hideous danger. In order to embody the three faces of the Goddess, I knew the three of us must face the maw of Botesh herself. My protectiveness made me secretive and deaf even to the counsel of my wisest advisors."* Shann rested her hand against Jess's face for a moment.

"I'm sorry you went through so much." Samantha's inherent kindness warmed her voice. *"But why are you so sure about us? When did you know?"*

"I first suspected when Brenna heard an immortal voice address her as 'j'heika,' Samantha." Shann smiled and returned to her chair by the hearth. *"It's an honorific, an old Amazon word for queen. That's how I learned Brenna would inherit my crown."*

"Which still has not been decided," Brenna put in. *"Or in any way agreed to, Sammy."*

"Hey, better you than me." Samantha nudged Brenna. *"I heard that 'j'heika' thing too."*

"Yes, Sam," Shann said. *"Your hearing that title confirmed my hopes. You and Brenna are both of the royal line."*

"But, Shann..." Brenna's head was starting to hurt, and Jess stood behind her and rested her hands on her shoulders. *"What royal line? I thought Tristaine's queens were chosen. You were. The crown doesn't pass from mother to daughter."*

"Except in times of Tristaine's greatest travail." Shann *leaned forward and took Brenna's hand. "Think back, Blades. Remember the scrolls of our Mothers and the promise Artemis made our clan."*

"Artemis..." Brenna frowned.

"When Tristaine is in deepest tribulation..."

"She will be led by three generations of blood-bonded queens," Jess recited. Brenna mouthed the words with her, remembering that spectral voice.

"Thank you, Jesstin." Shann smiled at her second. "This century presents tremendous challenge to our sisters. Artemis keeps Her word, adanin. I believe our reunion is goddess-sent."

"Shann. Wait." Brenna felt a bit dazed. "You're queen. And I'm your daughter. And you think I'm supposed to rule Tristaine after you. I'm still trying to wrap my head around that much, mind you. Now you're talking about a granddaughter. This is some future kid? A child Sammy or I might have?"

"Perhaps, Bren." Shann's gaze was on Samantha.

Samantha's face lost all expression. "My baby is dead, Shann."

"Brenna was told you were dead, Samantha. And I believed it of you both."

"And we're finished, Brenna."

Vona straightened and stepped back to examine the vibrant colors of the design etched at the base of Brenna's throat. The older woman's face was a fine webwork of wrinkles and laugh lines that deepened with her smile. "I hope you'll be pleased, honey."

"How could I not be?" Brenna stepped down from the high stool she had perched upon the last three hours, wincing at the stiffness in one hip. "You've drawn our clan's glyphs for forty years, grandmother."

"And no two alike." Vona's nimble fingers corked small vials of ink. "By the sound of things, they're almost ready for you out there, dear. Go on. See what your handsome adonai thinks of your sigil."

Brenna kissed Vona's cheek, then ducked out of the tent into the frosty night air.

The square was thronging with Amazons just beginning to settle into place for the covenant ceremony. It was the first time Tristaine had assembled in full since lighting the funeral pyres for her fallen warriors. Nineteen lost in all, a stunning toll. Tonight was the clan's first step out of grieving, a time to celebrate their salvation.

Six festive bonfires burned at intervals around the square, illuminating their gathering in a warm gold light. Brenna searched the crowd for Hakan and saw her resting against her wife's shoulder, cloaked in heavy furs. Shann had fought for Hakan's life over a series of three nights and only today released her from the healing lodge.

Samantha's light hair made her easier to spot. She sat with Vicar and Wai Li, cradling their son on her lap.

"That hurt like a sumbitch." Dana pulled her collar open and peered at the top of her shoulder. Her own glyph had been drawn just before Brenna's.

"Thank you." Brenna fanned her throat ruefully. "Repeat that in Jess's hearing, please. You ready for this, Dana?"

"Sure." Dana grinned down at her. "Couldn't be much spookier than wrangling with Botesh."

They strolled together toward the square. Shann stood in the center of the open space, near the blasted patch of ground that once had held the black altar. It was a benign and featureless plot now, a charred scar in the earth that bore no trace of menace. Tristaine's artisans were preparing a stone monument bearing the names of their dead to sanctify the spot.

CATE CULPEPPER

Brenna listened to the musical blend of hundreds of women's voices that filled the air with a benevolent murmur. Laughter appeared and faded like patches of sunlight in the crowd. Shann received the greetings and blessings of several Amazons before they sat on blankets and furs around the square. As if feeling her gaze, Shann turned toward Brenna and sent her a small, private smile.

Brenna smiled back. Shann had always evoked deep feelings in her, but now they were harder to classify. Brenna had never held illusions about her parentage. She was forced into adulthood so quickly, she'd had no time to romanticize a phantom mother and had little frame of reference for that bond now. Shann wasn't pushing her. She'd made it clear to both Brenna and Samantha that her door was open and her hearth kindled at all times.

Jess's reaction had infuriated her.

"Ah, makes sense?" Brenna repeated. "That's all you have to say?"

"Aye."

"Jesstin. What part of Shann, Queen of Tristaine, being my long-lost mother makes anything resembling sense to you?"

"I thought Shann had the most beautiful smile in the world, until I met you." Jess traced the curve of Brenna's lips with one finger. "You have our lady's light."

"I have our lady's DNA." Brenna perched her chin on Jess's sternum and contemplated the embers in the fireplace. The red glow was their small cabin's only illumination. "And I have a name for my father, Jess."

"That you do."

"Shann doesn't have any pictures of him. I wonder if seeing his face would tell me anything about his personality."

"You already know his heart, querida." Jess stroked

*Brenna's hair. "Your David earned the love of the wisest
woman we know. He fathered two fine daughters. And he'd be
richly proud of his eldest, Brenna."*

*"Jess." Brenna was touched. "Thank you." She kissed
the swell of Jess's shoulder.*

*"Your hand unleashed Tristaine's power, Bren. You've
earned the gratitude of the entire clan. And I'm learning,
finally, to share you with my sisters."*

*"Jesstin." Brenna lifted herself on one elbow and peered
down at Jess's firelit face. "What are you talking about?"*

*"You came to Tristaine as my adonai, lass." Jess lifted
Brenna's hand and fingered the silver bracelet encircling her
wrist. "You've grown into a true Amazon in your own right.
It's time you chose your glyph."*

*Brenna felt that truth resonate in her gut, and warmth
spread through her in a wave. She smiled and touched Jess's
face. "Yeah. It's time."*

"Uh-oh. Is this a trance?" Dana patted Brenna's head
gently.

"Nah. Just thinking." Brenna wrapped Dana's arm in
one of her own as they walked. "This ceremony tonight. It's
big, for me."

"It's big for me too. It's like becoming a nun."

Brenna sputtered.

"No, it is," Dana said. She waved at someone in the
sea of women around them. "We're turning away from all the
material stuff we grew up with, to live in a sisterhood for the
rest of our days. And we're pledging our fealty to something
bigger than us. In this case, Tristaine," she added.

"Hm." Brenna appraised Dana's open face with some-
thing like maternal affection. "Amazon as spiritual vocation.
Great topic for our next storyfire." She shook Dana's arm.
"It's the perfect time to welcome you to the clan, Dana. You're

already important to these women. Your courage in battle won a lot of respect around here."

"Yeah, about that." Dana faced Brenna and folded her arms. "Uh, thank you. You were nice to me before anybody else was, Brenna. You and Shann. And you had less reason to be nice to me than anyone. What with me tasering Jess in the gut and all. So thanks."

Brenna smiled up at Dana, then stood on her toes and kissed her cheek.

Dana grinned broadly. "You don't see that hulk of yours anywhere nearby, right?"

Brenna looked over Dana's shoulder directly into Jess's smiling eyes. "Nope, not a sign of her."

"Cool. See you out there." Dana turned and smacked bodily into Jess. "Dang!"

"Careful, youngster." Jess steadied her while Dana muttered something about dang mountains and lifted her hand from Dana's shoulder when she yelped. "Ah, sorry. I know it's sore. Can we see it?"

Dana closed her collar around her throat with an apologetic shrug. "Nah, not right now. I'll show you guys later."

"There's someone you want to show first," Brenna guessed.

"Yeah." Dana smiled. "I want her to see it first."

"As it should be." Jess clapped Dana on the butt. "Go find her, adanin. We'll be starting soon."

Brenna stepped into Jess's arms and leaned against her, grateful for her added warmth. They watched Kyla emerge from a group of seated Amazons and go to Dana.

"May I?" Jess touched Brenna's collar.

"Please." Brenna smiled. "I wanted you to be the first."

Jess opened her topshirt and bared the shining glyph above her breasts. Warm light ignited her eyes.

"Tell me," Brenna said softly.

"It's beautiful, lass. Colors like jewels." Her fingers drifted above the circular design. "The sign of the healer is here, cresting the field of the Seven Sisters. This bottom border is the gold plant that marks a seer." Jess grinned down at her. "I see no signet of royalty, however."

Brenna lifted her eyebrow, a gesture she knew mirrored Shann perfectly. "I design my own glyph, thank you."

"True enough," Jess agreed. She dipped her head and kissed her, a pleasant buzz that lingered, then deepened and grew heated. Brenna melted against Jess, and her hands snuck into her wild hair. They were both saved from public embarrassment only by Shann's soft call.

"Give witness, adanin!" Shann stood by the barren grave of their vanquished enemy. "Tonight we welcome two new sisters to Amazon Nation. Draw near and attend their covenants to Tristaine."

Jess raked her hair out of her eyes, caught her breath, and offered her arm to Brenna. Their first few steps into the square were slightly unsteady.

Kyla and Dana joined them, and the four women walked across the open space to join Shann as a ripple of greeting rose from the watching crowd.

"Are we ready, dear ones?" Shann raised a hand to welcome them to her side. Her eyes lingered on Brenna, and they were warm and proud. "Let's begin."

About the Author

Cate Culpepper is a 2005 Golden Crown Literary Award winner in the Sci-Fi/Fantasy category. She is the author of the Tristaine trilogy, which includes *Tristaine: The Clinic*, *Battle for Tristaine*, and *Tristaine Rises*. Cate grew up in southern New Mexico, where she served as the state lesbian for several years. She now resides in the Pacific Northwest with her faithful sidekick, Kirby, Warrior Westie. Cate supervises a transitional living program for homeless young gay adults. She can be reached at Klancy7@aol.com.

Books Available From Bold Strokes Books

Combust the Sun by Andrews & Austin. A Richfield and Rivers mystery set in L.A. Murder among the stars. (1-933110-52-X)

Of Drag Kings and the Wheel of Fate by Susan Smith. A blind date in a drag club leads to an unlikely romance. (1-933110-51-1)

Tristaine Rises by Cate Culpepper. Brenna, Jesstin, and the Amazons of Tristaine face their greatest challenge for survival. (1-933110-50-3)

Too Close to Touch by Georgia Beers. Kylie O'Brien believes in true love and is willing to wait for it. It doesn't matter one damn bit that Gretchen, her new and off-limits boss, has a voice as rich and smooth as melted chocolate. It absolutely doesn't. (1-933110-47-3)

The 100ᵗʰ Generation by Justine Saracen. Ancient curses, modern day villains, and a most intriguing woman who keeps appearing when least expected lead Archeologist Valerie Foret on the adventure of her life. (1-933110-48-1)

Battle for Tristaine by Cate Culpepper. While Brenna struggles to find her place in the clan and the love between her and Jess grows, Tristaine is threatened with destruction. Second in the Tristaine series. (1-933110-49-X)

The Traitor and the Chalice by Jane Fletcher. Without allies to help them, Tevi and Jemeryl will have to risk all in the race to uncover the traitor and retrieve the chalice. The Lyremouth Chronicles Book Two. (1-933110-43-0)

Promising Hearts by Radclyffe. Dr. Vance Phelps lost everything in the War Between the States and arrives in New Hope, Montana with no hope of happiness and no desire for anything except forgetting—until she meets Mae, a frontier madam. (1-933110-44-9)

Carly's Sound by Ali Vali. Poppy Valente and Julia Johnson form a bond of friendship that lays the foundation for something more, until Poppy's past comes back to haunt her—literally. A poignant romance about love and renewal. (1-933110-45-7)

Unexpected Sparks by Gina L. Dartt. Falling in love is complicated enough without adding murder to the mix. Kate Shannon's growing feelings for much younger Nikki Harris are challenging enough without the mystery of a fatal fire that Kate can't ignore. (1-933110-46-5)

Whitewater Rendezvous by Kim Baldwin. Two women on a wilderness kayak adventure—Chaz Herrick, a laid-back outdoorswoman, and Megan Maxwell, a workaholic news executive—discover that true love may be nothing at all like they imagined. (1-933110-38-4)

Erotic Interludes 3: Lessons in Love by Stacia Seaman and Radclyffe, eds. Sign on for a class in love…the best lesbian erotica writers take us to "school." (1-933110-39-2)

Punk Like Me by JD Glass. Twenty-one year old Nina writes lyrics and plays guitar in the rock band, Adam's Rib, and she doesn't always play by the rules. And, oh yeah—she has a way with the girls. (1-933110-40-6)

Coffee Sonata by Gun Brooke. Four women whose lives unexpectedly intersect in a small town by the sea share one thing in common—they all have secrets. (1-933110-41-4)

The Clinic: Tristaine Book One by Cate Culpepper. Brenna, a prison medic, finds herself deeply conflicted by her growing feelings for her patient, Jesstin, a wild and rebellious warrior reputed to be descended from ancient Amazons. (1-933110-42-2)

Forever Found by JLee Meyer. Can time, tragedy, and shattered trust destroy a love that seemed destined? When chance reunites two childhood friends separated by tragedy, the past resurfaces to determine the shape of their future. (1-933110-37-6)

Sword of the Guardian by Merry Shannon. Princess Shasta's bold new bodyguard has a secret that could change both of their lives. He is actually a *she*. A passionate romance filled with courtly intrigue, chivalry, and devotion. (1-933110-36-8)

Wild Abandon by Ronica Black. From their first tumultuous meeting, Dr. Chandler Brogan and Officer Sarah Monroe are drawn together by their common obsessions—sex, speed, and danger. (1-933110-35-X)

Turn Back Time by Radclyffe. Pearce Rifkin and Wynter Thompson have nothing in common but a shared passion for surgery. They clash at every opportunity, especially when matters of the heart are suddenly at stake. (1-933110-34-1)

Chance by Grace Lennox. At twenty-six, Chance Delaney decides her life isn't working so she swaps it for a different one. What follows is the sexy, funny, touching story of two women who, in finding themselves, also find one another. (1-933110-31-7)

The Exile and the Sorcerer by Jane Fletcher. First in the Lyremouth Chronicles. Tevi, wounded and adrift, arrives in the courtyard of a shy young sorcerer. Together they face monsters, magic, and the challenge of loving despite their differences. (1-933110-32-5)

A Matter of Trust by Radclyffe. JT Sloan is a cybersleuth who doesn't like attachments. Michael Lassiter is leaving her husband, and she needs Sloan's expertise to safeguard her company. It should just be business—but it turns into much more. (1-933110-33-3)

Sweet Creek by Lee Lynch. A celebration of the enduring nature of love, friendship, and community in the quirky, heart-warming lesbian community of Waterfall Falls. (1-933110-29-5)

The Devil Inside by Ali Vali. Derby Cain Casey, head of a New Orleans crime organization, runs the family business with guts and grit, and no one crosses her. No one, that is, until Emma Verde claims her heart and turns her world upside down. (1-933110-30-9)

Grave Silence by Rose Beecham. Detective Jude Devine's investigation of a series of ritual murders is complicated by her torrid affair with the golden girl of Southwestern forensic pathology, Dr. Mercy Westmoreland. (1-933110-25-2)

Honor Reclaimed by Radclyffe. In the aftermath of 9/11, Secret Service Agent Cameron Roberts and Blair Powell close ranks with a trusted few to find the would-be assassins who nearly claimed Blair's life. (1-933110-18-X)

Honor Bound by Radclyffe. Secret Service Agent Cameron Roberts and Blair Powell face political intrigue, a clandestine threat to Blair's safety, and the seemingly irreconcilable personal differences that force them ever farther apart. (1-933110-20-1)

Protector of the Realm: Supreme Constellations Book One by Gun Brooke. A space adventure filled with suspense and a daring intergalactic romance featuring Commodore Rae Jacelon and a stunning, but decidedly lethal, Kellen O'Dal. (1-933110-26-0)

Innocent Hearts by Radclyffe. In a wild and unforgiving land, two women learn about love, passion, and the wonders of the heart. (1-933110-21-X)

The Temple at Landfall by Jane Fletcher. An imprinter, one of Celaeno's most revered servants of the Goddess, is also a prisoner to the faith—until a Ranger frees her by claiming her heart. The Celaeno series. (1-933110-27-9)

Force of Nature by Kim Baldwin. From tornados to forest fires, the forces of nature conspire to bring Gable McCoy and Erin Richards close to danger, and closer to each other. (1-933110-23-6)

In Too Deep by Ronica Black. Undercover homicide cop Erin McKenzie tracks a femme fatale who just might be a real killer…with love and danger hot on her heels. (1-933110-17-1)

Erotic Interludes 2: Stolen Moments by Stacia Seaman and Radclyffe, eds. Love on the run, in the office, in the shadows…Fast, furious, and almost too hot to handle. (1-933110-16-3)

Course of Action by Gun Brooke. Actress Carolyn Black desperately wants the starring role in an upcoming film produced by Annelie Peterson. Just how far will she go for the dream part of a lifetime? (1-933110-22-8)

Rangers at Roadsend by Jane Fletcher. Sergeant Chip Coppelli has learned to spot trouble coming, and that is exactly what she sees in her new recruit, Katryn Nagata. The Celaeno series. (1-933110-28-7)

Justice Served by Radclyffe. Lieutenant Rebecca Frye and her lover, Dr. Catherine Rawlings, embark on a deadly game of hide-and-seek with an underworld kingpin who traffics in human souls. (1-933110-15-5)

Distant Shores, Silent Thunder by Radclyffe. Doctor Tory King—and the women who love her—is forced to examine the boundaries of love, friendship, and the ties that transcend time. (1-933110-08-2)

Hunter's Pursuit by Kim Baldwin. A raging blizzard, a mountain hideaway, and a killer-for-hire set a scene for disaster—or desire—when Katarzyna Demetrious rescues a beautiful stranger. (1-933110-09-0)

The Walls of Westernfort by Jane Fletcher. All Temple Guard Natasha Ionadis wants is to serve the Goddess—until she falls in love with one of the rebels she is sworn to destroy. The Celaeno series. (1-933110-24-4)

Erotic Interludes: *Change of Pace* by Radclyffe. Twenty-five hot-wired encounters guaranteed to spark more than just your imagination. Erotica as you've always dreamed of it. (1-933110-07-4)

Honor Guards by Radclyffe. In a wild flight for their lives, the president's daughter and those who are sworn to protect her wage a desperate struggle for survival. (1-933110-01-5)

Justice in the Shadows by Radclyffe. In a shadow world of secrets and lies, Detective Sergeant Rebecca Frye and her lover, Dr. Catherine Rawlings, join forces in the elusive search for justice.(1-933110-03-1)

Love & Honor by Radclyffe. The president's daughter and her lover are faced with difficult choices as they battle a tangled web of Washington intrigue for...love and honor. (1-933110-10-4)

Beyond the Breakwater by Radclyffe. One Provincetown summer three women learn the true meaning of love, friendship, and family. (1-933110-06-6)

Tomorrow's Promise by Radclyffe. One timeless summer, two very different women discover the power of passion to heal and the promise of hope that only love can bestow. (1-933110-12-0)

Love's Melody Lost by Radclyffe. A secretive artist with a haunted past and a young woman escaping a life that has proved to be a lie find their destinies entwined. (1-933110-00-7)

Safe Harbor by Radclyffe. A mysterious newcomer, a reclusive doctor, and a troubled gay teenager learn about love, friendship, and trust during one tumultuous summer in Provincetown. (1-933110-13-9)

Above All, Honor by Radclyffe. Secret Service Agent Cameron Roberts fights her desire for the one woman she can't have—Blair Powell, the daughter of the president of the United States. (1-933110-04-X)